A Bitter Homecoming

THE DRIZZLE BECAME A DOWNPOUR as the barge approached the Water Gate. This gate was the one to which my mother had been brought, in this same manner, eighteen years earlier. I wept, thinking of how she had never left. I was following in the footsteps of many who had been accused of treason and whose last steps from freedom toward death had begun at this exact spot.

"Take me to another gate, any gate but this!" I cried. But the guards stared straight ahead, refusing to hear.

As I stepped from the barge, all strength drained from my legs, which gave way under me. Overcome by terror, I collapsed onto the stone steps, which were wet from the lapping river. I lay crumpled in the rain, unable to go another step. The warders of the Tower sent to meet me stared down at me. I gazed up at them, searching for a sympathetic face. I felt utterly without hope.

Then one, followed by another, abruptly stepped out of the formation, cried, "God preserve Your Grace!" and knelt before me. Immediately others of the warders seized me roughly, set me upon my feet, and ordered me to enter the Tower.

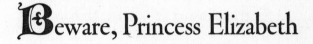

Beware, Princess Elizabeth

A YOUNG ROYALS BOOK

Beware, Princess Elizabeth

CAROLYN MEYER

Gulliver Books
Harcourt, Inc.
San Diego   New York   London

www.HarcourtBooks.com

First Gulliver Books paperback edition 2002
First published 2001
Gulliver Books is a trademark of Harcourt, Inc., registered in the United States of America and/or other jurisdictions.

The Library of Congress has cataloged the hardcover edition as follows:
Meyer, Carolyn.
Beware, Princess Elizabeth/Carolyn Meyer.
p.   cm.
"Gulliver Books."
Summary: After the death of her father, King Henry VIII, in 1547, thirteen-year-old Elizabeth must endure the political intrigues and dangers of the reigns of her half-brother Edward and her half-sister Mary before finally becoming Queen of England eleven years later.
1. Elizabeth I, Queen of England, 1533–1603—Childhood and youth—Juvenile fiction. 2. Great Britain—History—Edward VI and Mary, 1547–1558—Juvenile fiction. [1. Elizabeth I, Queen of England, 1533–1603—Childhood and youth—Fiction. 2. Great Britain—History—Edward VI and Mary, 1547–1558—Fiction. 3. Mary I, Queen of England, 1516–1558—Fiction. 4. Princesses—Fiction. 5. Sisters—Fiction.] I. Title.
PZ7.M5685Be   2001
[Fic]—dc21   00-11700
ISBN 0-15-202659-2
ISBN 0-15-204556-2 pb

Text set in Spectrum
Designed by Lydia D'moch

A C E G H F D B

For Elizabeth Van Doren—
inspiration, archeditor, and friend

Ferdinand and Isabella
of Spain

Henry VII
and Elizabeth of York

Catherine of Aragon ———— MARRIED 1501 ———— Arthur
(1485–1536)   (1486–1502)

MARRIED 1509
MARRIAGE ANNULLED 1533

Henry
(born and died 1511)

Mary Tudor — Philip II,
(1516–1558)   of Spain
(1527–1598)

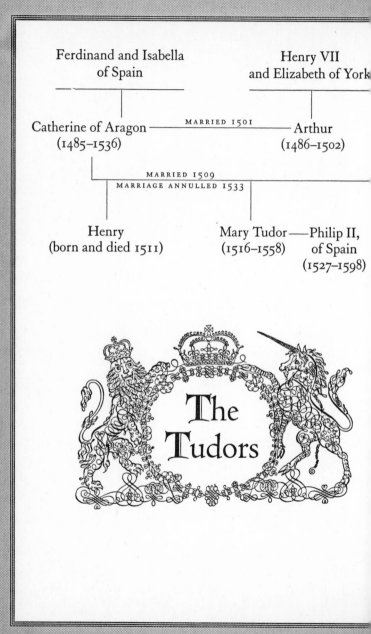

The
Tudors

Henry VIII
(1491–1547)

NEVER MARRIED — Elizabeth (Bessie) Blount
(1502?–1539)

Henry Fitzroy
(1519–1536)

MARRIED 1533 — Anne Boleyn
(1507?–1536)

Elizabeth
(1533–1603)

MARRIED 1536 — Jane Seymour
(1509–1537)

Edward VI
(1537–1553)

MARRIED 1540
MARRIAGE ANNULLED 1540 — Anne of Cleves
(1515–1557)

MARRIED 1540 — Catherine Howard
(1520?–1542)

MARRIED 1543 — Catherine Parr
(1512–1548)

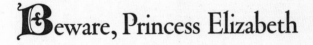

Beware, Princess Elizabeth

PROLOGUE

Hatfield, Hertfordshire, England
17 November 1558

THERE WAS A TIME, long ago, that I loved my sister. There may have been a time that Mary loved me. But that all changed. It had to, given who we were: the daughters of Henry VIII. Our father at times adored us but often shunned us and occasionally nearly forgot us. We were not the sons he desired.

Worse: I am the daughter of the woman Mary hated most in the world. She never forgave me for who my mother was: Anne Boleyn, who took the place of Mary's mother as queen.

When I was born Mary was forced to be my servant—not an easy thing for a proud young woman of seventeen. How she must have loathed that! But then, before I reached my third birthday, my mother was dead, her execution ordered by my own father—and Mary's.

Yet, in spite of all, it seemed for a time that Mary was truly fond of me—before she turned bitter, before she recognized that we were enemies.

My path to the throne has been long and fraught with peril. Now I am ready to follow in the footsteps of my father, England's greatest king. Mary, who hindered me at every turn, will soon be forgotten. But I promise you, history will remember me, Elizabeth, not for who my father was, or my mother or my sister, but for myself.

CHAPTER I

The Death
of My Father

"The king is dead."

Those four words, cold as marble and sharp as flint, were uttered by the thin, cruel lips of Edward Seymour, the king's privy councillor and my brother's uncle. In this way I learned of my father's death. The date was the thirty-first of January, *anno Domini* 1547.

My father, dead! I knew that he had been ill, yet the news still came as a terrible shock. It seemed impossible that the great King Henry would no longer stride like a giant through the kingdom and through my life. I was not close to him, and I had spent little time with him in the years of my growing up. Nevertheless, he had been an enormous presence in my life. Now, suddenly, my father was gone. I would have neither his protection nor his occasional bursts of affection. I was alone, and—I confess it—I was afraid.

But I had no time to dwell on my own tumultuous feelings. My brother burst into tears at the news and threw himself sobbing into my arms. Named Edward in honor of this uncle, he was nine years old, a beautiful boy, delicate as a wren's egg. I held him, and my own tears fell upon his thick curls. I was thirteen, poised on the brink of womanhood, but at that moment I felt like a child myself. My brother and I were orphans, and now he was king. I can scarcely imagine his terror.

"When did my father die?" I asked Seymour, struggling to still the tremor in my voice.

"On the morning of the twenty-eighth."

"Three days past?" I asked sharply. "Why am I told only now?"

"There were decisions to be made," Seymour replied in a cold voice. "For three days no one but members of the privy council was informed of the king's death."

I glared at him. I did not trust Seymour, even then. *Decisions concerning what?* I wanted to ask boldly, but I did not, for I saw that my questions angered him.

Seymour was the brother of young Edward's mother, Jane Seymour, who had died soon after giving birth to my brother. Seymour had made himself so much part of our family that he'd carried me in Edward's christening procession. Now he was the most powerful of the privy councillors. Seymour had his own reasons for keeping the death of the king of England a secret. I guessed that it was to make sure of his own power over the new king.

Instead of demanding an explanation, I asked merely, "Has my sister, Mary, been informed?"

"She has," he snapped. "Madam, your questions could delay our arrival in London. Kindly summon your servants. We must leave at once."

"You have waited three days to tell us of our father's death," I retorted. "Now, if you please, have the kindness to allow me a little time to console my brother, the king." Without waiting for a reply, I knelt beside the sobbing, quivering boy. Only when he was somewhat soothed and my own feelings calmed did I call for Kat Ashley to prepare for our journey.

"LORD HAVE MERCY!" Kat cried out when I told her the news. She put on a great show of wailing and blubbering that I only half believed. Kat had been my governess and dearest confidante since I was three years old. We knew each other very well, and I sensed that although she deemed it proper to grieve for the death of the monarch, she could not forgive my father for his treatment of my mother and for the many times he seemed to have forgotten me. While Kat continued her lamentations, I summoned the maids of the chamber to begin laying out the black mourning garments I would need.

Eventually—not quickly enough for Seymour, but in good time—our belongings were packed into panniers carried by horses, and our mounts prepared. Frost crunched beneath the horses' hooves as we plodded along rutted roadways. For once Kat was mostly silent, and I was finally able to give myself over to my grief.

I hadn't seen my father for two years, since last he called me to court to celebrate the dawning of the new year. That was how he was—sometimes I was in the king's favor, sometimes not. It had been this way all my life. For a time he hadn't even acknowledged me as his daughter, long ago declaring both my sister, Mary, and me bastards. (Mary is the child of his first wife, I of his second, and Edward of his third.) Yet, only weeks before his death, I learned that he had restored us to the succession, putting us in line for the throne after Edward and whatever children my father's only son would produce. My sister and I were still bastards, but we were the king's heirs. I stood a long way from the throne, however, and it did not once occur to me that day as I rode toward London that I might one day become queen.

IT WAS LATE afternoon, and the torches were already lit when we reached London. We were chilled to the bone and aching with weariness. But we could not rest. We had to hasten at once to Whitehall Palace, where my father's body lay in state in the chapel. His enormous coffin was surrounded by dozens of mourners and as many flickering candles. As I entered the chapel, I gave a start and nearly cried out, for beside the coffin stood a wax effigy of the king, dressed in magnificent jeweled robes. The extremely lifelike figure didn't resemble my pain-wracked father as I last saw him. It was made to portray the king in his vigorous youth. I had never seen him like this. My earliest memories were of a man who was already turned fat and ungainly. I was unprepared for the feelings of loss and yearning that swept through me for the awesomely powerful man I had never known.

Near the coffin sat Queen Catherine, my father's sixth wife, pale but composed. It would be wrong to describe her as beautiful, for Catherine, at thirty-four, was past her bloom. But she had a kindness in her eyes and a generous mouth that, on less somber occasions, smiled easily. I thought how lonely she would now be without my father. She had been so attentive to him in his last months, when he was feeble and in pain. He had been a demanding husband, yet she was sure to feel his absence keenly.

By her side sat one of our cousins, Lady Jane Grey, gently stroking the queen's hand. As we entered, Jane jumped to her feet, and she and Edward rushed weeping into each other's arms. I stood silently by, observing the scene. I, too, felt like weeping, but I would never reveal my feelings so easily.

After Edward received Queen Catherine's embrace, it was my turn. I stepped forward and knelt before her, and when she raised me up I kissed her with true affection. As I did so I noticed the man who hovered near her chair with an air of solicitude. He gazed at me, and I couldn't help gazing back frankly. Two years previous, when I was last at court, I had met Tom Seymour, brother of Edward Seymour and another of my little brother's uncles. I'd paid little attention to him then— I was but a child of eleven. But now thirteen and aware of such things, I was quite conscious of his eyes lingering upon me.

Tom Seymour was tall, at least six feet, although not so tall as my father, with a slender, athletic build. His dark hair fell over his brow, and his beard was red and abundant. His brown eyes generally glowed with merriment, although at times they seemed to smolder with less pleasant emotions. I thought him very handsome.

After gazing at me for a long moment, he bowed and greeted me cordially, expressing his deep sympathy. But almost immediately he turned to my brother with an outpouring of affection. Edward had been weeping more or less steadily since Seymour brought us the news. Now he suddenly brightened and fairly leaped into Tom's arms. Tom swept up the frail boy in an embrace that nearly engulfed him.

At that moment Edward Seymour stepped forward. "Set him down at once," he ordered Tom in a tone that brooked no refusal. "This is the king of England, you fool! Not some idle toy for your pleasure!"

The two Seymours stared at each other while my brother clung to Tom like a cub to its dam. Then, very gently, Tom set the young king on his feet again and knelt before him. "Your Majesty," Tom said reverently. Edward Seymour cast his brother a scornful look and turned away.

What interested me even more than the anger that flashed between the two men was something in the eyes of Queen Catherine. She gazed at Tom Seymour with an expression that could mean only one thing: *She loves him.*

At once I wondered: *How long has she loved him? My father has been dead for less than a week!* This realization troubled me; I cared for Queen Catherine, and I could not bear to think of her as a disloyal wife. My mind raced on: *And what of Tom Seymour? Does he love the queen?*

I WAS KNEELING in prayer by my father's coffin when my sister, Mary, arrived. Her entrance created a considerable stir. Unless we were called to court, we rarely saw each other, although we lived only half a day's journey apart and often exchanged politely formal letters.

I was surprised at how she looked. She would be thirty-one in a few days, but she appeared much older. Her skin was blanched, her face pinched, her once red-gold hair now faded and thin. She seemed shrunken inside her mourning clothes, and yet she glittered from head to foot with diamonds and pearls. In her love of jewels, at least, she resembled our father! We greeted each other as daughters of the king, as the occasion demanded, and wept in each other's arms. Yet there was no warmth in our embrace. We were not enemies then, but neither were we friends. For my part I felt no more than if I had been embracing a near-stranger.

As Mary and I stood by our father's bier, I recalled the summer our father had wed Catherine. After the marriage ceremony at Hampton Court in July of 1543, Mary and I, and Edward, had accompanied the bridal couple on a honeymoon progress through the countryside. Each summer my father made a royal progress to let himself be seen by his subjects, stopping for a week or a fortnight with noble families along the way and amusing himself each day with hunting. The purpose of this progress was to display his new wife as well as to hunt for deer.

No one paid me much attention that summer except Catherine, who was quite gracious to me. I was grateful for her kindness, for as a nine-year-old girl I did not like to be ignored. Wherever we went, little Edward, curly haired and adorable heir to the throne, was of course the object of much cooing and petting. But it was my sister, Mary, who received enthusiastic greetings from the crowds that turned out to hail us as we rode through hamlets and villages. This seemed to annoy my father, who took to teasing Mary about finding her a husband.

"Twenty-seven and still a virgin!" he would roar. "Perhaps I know of a German prince who would have you as his wife!" Then later it would be the French dauphin, or some Danish count. He teased her as one might taunt a dog with a bone.

"As my lord wishes," Mary would reply in her deep, almost manly voice, taking care not to show her hurt or embarrassment.

Mary might have hidden her true feelings from our father, but I caught a glimpse of them one day when we stopped to rest by the side of a stream. Our servants rushed about, setting up planks on trestles beneath the branches of a large oak. While our meal was being laid out, I saw Mary wander off alone along the banks of the stream. My father's leg was paining him, as it often did, and Catherine was busy tending to his needs. Edward had fallen asleep on the couch brought for him. Partly out of boredom and partly, I suppose, out of jealousy that she was the favored sister—my father didn't even bother to tease me—I decided to follow Mary and to spy on her. What I thought I would witness I cannot say.

After a time her footsteps slowed, then stopped. She flung herself down on the grassy bank and burst into tears. I watched from behind a tree as she sobbed as though her heart were breaking. Part of me wanted to flee back to the royal company, where perhaps I might now receive some of my father's attention. But Mary's grief touched something within me, and after a time I stepped out from my hiding place. I didn't know what to say, and so I simply stood where she might notice me.

When Mary realized that she was not alone, she stifled a startled cry. "Yes?" she asked irritably. "What is it, Elizabeth?"

"You seem so sad," I said.

Mary gazed at me thoughtfully. "I am twenty-seven years old. I have neither husband nor child, nor any hope of one. It is a terrible thing to live without love, Elizabeth."

"I love you, dearest sister," I murmured, and I moved to lay my hand softly upon her cheek.

"You!" she said harshly, pulling back, and I stepped away in surprise. "You!"

Stung, I turned and ran back to join the others. The board was laid with a meal of meat pasties and fish pudding and ale, but I had no appetite. Soon Mary joined us, her eyes puffed and reddened. My father noticed nothing, but I saw the new queen observing Mary carefully. Feeling rebuffed, I avoided Mary as much as I could for the rest of our journey. It was not difficult to do, for she seemed to avoid me as well.

When the royal progress ended at the close of summer, each of us returned to our homes. Mary went to her manor house at Hunsdon in Hertfordshire, north of London. Edward was taken to his palace at Ashridge and I to Hatfield Palace, also in Hertfordshire, accompanied by our various tutors and governesses. The king and queen returned to my father's favorite palace at Greenwich, on the River Thames, east of London. For a time I missed them, until I got caught up again in my studies and thought less and less of my family.

Since then I had seen little of the new couple or of Mary, except when we all were invited to court for Yuletide and New Year's, again at Easter, and once more at Whitsuntide. On those occasions I was careful not to approach Mary closely, no matter how genial she may have appeared. But now, at my father's funeral, I had no choice. I wondered what my sister's thoughts were as we stood side by side, her fingers entwined with mine.

CHAPTER 2

Edward the King

The body of King Henry lay in state for twelve days. During the long hours that I was required to kneel beside his coffin, I had much time to think back upon my relationship with my father.

"You remind him of your mother," Kat once said when I complained that he paid me no attention. "Nothing will change that." And nothing did. He never spoke of it, of course. It was forbidden to utter the name of Anne Boleyn. It was as if my mother had never existed. Every trace of her had been removed—every trace, that is, but me.

I owe my understanding of my father and my mother to dear Kat. Night after night, as we lay side by side in the darkness with the bed curtains drawn closed around us, it was Kat who whispered answers to my deepest questions. Sometimes I asked about my father and often about my mother. Kat is the only person with whom I ever spoke of Anne Boleyn.

"She was beautiful, with hair black as a raven's wing and eyes black as jet, and she was intelligent and witty as well," Kat would say of my mother. "She fascinated your father from the first time he set eyes upon her."

She fascinated him, but he already had a wife: Catherine of Aragon, who was Mary's mother. I learned, when I grew older, that my father had had his marriage to Catherine annulled in order to marry Anne. That first Catherine (three of my father's wives were named Catherine) did everything in her power to prevent the annulment. But my father banished Catherine, and Mary, too, to force her to consent to it. Yet, to her dying hour, even after my father had married Anne Boleyn and made her his queen, Catherine of Aragon refused her consent. Perhaps Mary had inherited from her mother that same stubbornness.

According to Kat my father believed Anne Boleyn would give him the son that poor old Catherine could not. To his great disappointment I, the only child of his marriage to Anne, was not a son. I was Anne's failure. When he no longer loved her, he determined to rid himself of her. He had her locked in the Tower and then contrived to have her sentenced to death for charges of adultery and treason. There was not a word of truth in the charges.

Would King Henry have ordered my mother's execution if I had been a boy? I believe not. He might have found love with another woman, as he was wont to do, but he would have let Anne live, and I would have had my mother. And so my feelings about my father were never simple and uncomplicated. I did love him, because he was my father and a great king. But I also harbored a dark secret: I resented him deeply for depriving me of my mother. The darkest secret of all: At times I hated him.

Then, just weeks after my mother's death, my father married Jane Seymour. "The opposite of your mother," Kat replied when I pressed her for a description of a woman I scarcely remember. "Pretty, I suppose, but rather colorless. Quite prim." Kat pursed her lips. "Queen Jane had the good fortune to bear a male child, to the king's delight. And then she had the good sense to die almost at once, before he tired of her."

Kat should never have said such a thing, of course, but Kat had a talent for saying things she ought not. Her tongue often brought her trouble.

My mother was not the only wife my father sent to the Tower and then had put to death. I was eight years old when his fifth, Catherine Howard, was sentenced to die. All the nervous excitement of this latest execution could not be kept from me, and it was as if my own mother's execution were being repeated. I wept, I cried out, for days I could neither sleep nor eat. Kat, frantic to calm me, summoned the court physician to prescribe a sleeping draught.

When I awoke it was over. I listened as servants whispered how Catherine Howard's head had been caught in a basket, her blood sopped up by crones with handkerchiefs, her body carried off for burial. *The way it must have been for my mother,* I thought, and I have thought of it many times since that day. Remembering Catherine Howard's death has always struck terror to my heart.

THE TWELVE DAYS of the lying-in-state ended. From the palace window Edward and Mary and I watched the somber procession that stretched for miles, following my father's coffin to Windsor Castle. By custom the monarch's heirs did not attend his funeral, but it seemed that nearly everyone else did. The wax effigy rode in a carriage drawn by eight black horses in black velvet trappings.

In the days that followed, I waited to learn what turn my life would take next. I had no control over events; I could only control my response to them. Wrapped in the silence of my own lonely thoughts, I paced the snowy paths in the bleak palace garden. My father was dead. My sister, Mary, was cold and withdrawn. My little brother, Edward, was now king. *What will become of me?* I wondered over and over. *What will become of me?* But I decided that, however much fear and worry now gnawed at my vitals, I would one day learn to rule my own life.

ON THE TWENTIETH day of February, *anno Domini* 1547, I witnessed the coronation of my brother, Edward. Those who were there the day in 1509 when my father was crowned were determined that this celebration would surpass it in grandeur.

The day before the coronation, as the royal procession wound its way through London, trumpeters blew fanfares to proclaim the approach of the boy-king. My little brother, dressed in cloth of silver embroidered in gold and belted with rubies, pearls, and diamonds, was mounted high on a huge white horse trapped with crimson satin. He was followed by the nobility of the kingdom, according to rank. The two Seymour brothers, Edward and Tom, took the lead.

So much splendor on such a delicate young boy! He wore a look of proud hauteur, but I knew that was a mask to disguise his fear. For a little while I imagined myself in his place, arrayed in ermine and jewels, surrounded by members of the privy council in their rich velvet robes. Henchmen carrying gilded poleaxes and knights in purple satin riding fine horses would precede my royal litter.

But I was not the queen, and short of a miracle I would never be queen. I was assigned a place far back in the procession, behind my sister, Mary, who sat in a chariot with Dowager Queen Catherine, the highest-ranking woman in the kingdom. Beside me rode Anne of Cleves, my father's fourth wife, a German princess my father had decided to wed seven years earlier on the basis of a small portrait he'd seen.

Anne of Cleves had spoken only German when she'd stepped off the ship that brought her to Dover. She was stoutly built, her skin pockmarked, her gowns and headdresses drearily old-fashioned. The king immediately saw that the flesh-and-blood woman did not match the portrait, much less his dreams of her, but he married her anyway. Six months later he had the marriage annulled—and sent to the gallows his chief secretary, Cromwell, who had arranged the match. Since the divorce Anne had had the status of "the king's sister" and had lived comfortably in one of the country houses he had given her with plenty of jewels and money to soothe her injured feelings. We were often paired at official occasions. We were fond of each other, and I was glad for her company. We were two women, one old and one young, who counted for little in the kingdom. Anne may not have cared, but I confess that I did. I was the trueborn daughter of King Henry VIII!

That night Edward slept in the Tower of London, traditional for each monarch in the history of England, including my mother, who spent the night there before her crowning as queen. It amuses me to think that I was present for that event, less than three months before my birth, riding in her belly, beneath all her jeweled finery.

But now my thoughts were not of Edward's coronation, but of another matter entirely that had been troubling me for days: the look I had seen Queen

Catherine bestow upon Tom Seymour. I knew that Kat would speak forthrightly once I had found a way to introduce the subject.

That night we retired to the chambers assigned to us. All but one of the candles were extinguished, and we climbed onto the high bed and drew the curtains against the cold. Our servants slept.

"Tom Seymour and the queen . . . ," I began hesitantly.

"She was in love with him before, you see," said Kat, almost as though she had read my thoughts. "Catherine has been in love with Tom Seymour these many years, since long before she married King Henry. And who can blame her? Do you not think him extraordinarily handsome?"

The handsomest I have ever seen, I thought. Aloud I said, "I scarcely noticed," and feigned a yawn. Then, "Will they wed, then, do you think?"

"The dowager queen must first complete a year of official mourning," said Kat. "We shall see if she lasts six months."

With that Kat rolled onto her side and fell fast asleep, leaving me to lie awake pondering this bit of news.

THE NEXT MORNING, after a solemn procession from the Tower to Westminster Abbey, the coronation commenced, hours of pomp and ceremony that left everyone exhausted. By evening the celebrants had recovered sufficiently, and the revelry began at Whitehall Palace, the new king's official residence.

Throughout the banquet no one paid me the least attention, as usual. I was seated far down the table from King Edward and completely ignored, as only a thirteen-year-old princess of lowly status can be ignored in the vast sea of dukes and duchesses, marquises and marchionesses, earls and countesses, barons and baronesses. But when the dancing began, my old friend Robin Dudley suddenly appeared at my side.

Robin had shared lessons with Edward and me and our tutors when Robin and I were eight years old—our birthdays are within days of each other. He was a merry lad then, as good-looking as he was good-humored, but I had not seen him in some time. Now thirteen, no longer a boy but not yet a man, he had the same bright eyes, reddish brown hair, and quick smile that I remembered well. He approached me shyly, but as soon as we joined the other dancers, his shyness vanished.

The dance was my favorite—lavolta, in which the partners take turns lifting each other off the floor. Of course, the lady does no actual lifting; the gentleman first executes a leap and then seizes the lady by the waist and propels her high into the air. When finally we stopped, breathless and laughing, Robin brought me a cup of hippocras and begged me to tell him where my life was taking me.

"I cannot say, Robin," I told him frankly as we sipped the spiced wine. "I am the king's daughter, but I think they have all forgotten me."

"I have not," he said, suddenly serious and taking my hand. "I shall never forget you, Elizabeth."

The passion with which he uttered this promise startled me, for I'd always thought of him as a brother. Yet his tone as well as his words held my attention. "Nor shall I forget you," I said.

I was happy passing the time with my old friend. But to my surprise, Tom Seymour appeared and claimed me for the next dance, a grave and stately pavane. I had felt lighthearted and at ease with Robin Dudley, but my feet turned to lumps of clay and my hands were cold as fish when I was on Tom Seymour's arm. I wanted to hide from embarrassment, and at the same time I wanted the dance to go on and on. The attraction I felt for this man was strong, the strongest I had ever experienced, and I sensed that he was drawn to me as well. But I knew the attraction was improper, even dangerous.

Later, when I looked again for Robin, he had disappeared. Then Kat materialized and announced that it would be wise for me to retire. "King Edward has long departed for his bedchamber," she said, frowning at me, "and so must you, madam."

I blamed the fireworks and booming cannons for keeping me awake until dawn. In truth the faces of a handsome man and a handsome boy troubled my sleep.

CHAPTER 3

The Lord Admiral

The day after Edward's coronation, Dowager Queen Catherine, my father's widow, astonished me with an invitation to come live with her at Chelsea Palace in London. "I would be happy for your company, Elizabeth," she said, "and it would give me great pleasure to continue to oversee your education. What do you say? Are you in agreement?"

"Oh yes, my lady Catherine!" I said, for I was fond of my stepmother.

London was noisy and dirty, unlike my quiet country home at Hatfield, where the only noise came from flocks of sheep in the nearby fields. But London was also exciting.

In preparation for the move from Hatfield, Kat bustled from chamber to chamber, giving orders to the serving maids. Now and again she paused to smile broadly at me.

"To London, to London!" she fairly sang. "Such a life you shall now have, madam!"

The maids were packing my chemises, my petticoats, my kirtles and gowns, my shoes and stockings and boots—all now too short, too tight, or too worn or threadbare—into wooden trunks. Kat looked first at a blue velvet gown she was holding in her hands and then at me. "You need a new gown, or two or three. You have grown at least a hand span since this one was made for you. I shall speak to Mr. Parry about it."

Thomas Parry, a puffed-up little Welshman, was my cofferer, in charge of the allowance that my father used to send for the upkeep of my household. His sister, Blanche Parry, a plainspoken and practical woman, was also in my service. Blanche and Kat had always complained there were not enough funds to provide properly for the king's younger daughter, although there always seemed to be plenty for his elder daughter, Mary. I wondered if that might now change with my brother on the throne.

On a wintry day in early March, under clouds heavy with snow, Kat and I and a small retinue of servants once again set out for London. Thick mud sucked at the horses' hooves, slowing our pace.

"Does my sister know of this change?" I asked Kat.

"Why, I have no idea, Elizabeth," Kat said. "Did you not write to her?"

I'd thought of sending word to Mary to inform her of my whereabouts, but in the commotion of the past weeks, I had neglected to do so. But then, I thought, neither had Mary taken the time to write to me. *Later,* I decided; *when I am settled, then I shall write.*

And I promptly forgot about her.

OUR WELCOME at the queen's beautiful Chelsea Palace was as warm as one could wish for. Queen Catherine didn't wait for me to beg her to receive me, but as soon as she had word of our arrival, she stepped out into the snowy courtyard to greet me. "How happy I am you have come to be with me," she said with an affectionate embrace.

She led Kat and me through elegant halls with marble floors and walls paneled in oak to our own apartments, a spacious suite of chambers with windows overlooking the River Thames. After inviting us to join her at supper when we were ready, the queen left us to recover from our journey.

As servants carried in our trunks and boxes, Kat went about examining everything from the candles in the sconces on the wall ("Good quality beeswax," she said approvingly) to the tester bed, with its canopy and curtains of heavy blue damask. "Look!" Kat whispered, poking her finger into the lofty bedding with its coverlet, also of blue. "Three mattresses, all well stuffed with wool."

I took more interest in a small writing desk, intricately carved, with two wooden stools covered in leather. There was even a supply of goose quills and a knife to sharpen them, and a little inkhorn. A cozy fire crackled on the hearth. I felt that I should be content here.

After we had rested, cleansed our hands and faces, and changed our muddy petticoats for fresh ones, we made our way to the gallery. Fine tapestries lined the walls. At one end, in a place of honor, hung a portrait of my father. Nearby was a smaller portrait of my grandfather, King Henry VII. I stood gazing into the eyes of the two portraits and tried to imagine what those great kings might have been thinking as the artist painted their images. Then a servant in livery of green and white, the Tudor colors, appeared and announced that the dowager queen awaited us in her private apartments.

The servant pushed open a heavy door. I entered the queen's privy chamber, ready to kneel before Catherine. But before I could do so, I found myself enveloped in the arms of Tom Seymour. I barely managed to suppress a startled cry.

"Welcome, dear sister Elizabeth!" he roared, and twirled me around before setting me down rather unsteadily on my feet. All of my life I had been carefully schooled in royal deportment, and so I was shocked at his behavior. At the same time, I confess, I was also thrilled.

I looked with alarm from this handsome, boisterous man to the sweet, smiling countenance of my step-mother. Queen Catherine must have observed my confusion, for she immediately took care to present him formally: "Thomas Seymour, baron of Sudeley."

What are you doing here? I thought, but I made a curtsy and murmured a bit breathlessly, "My lord."

The baron bowed deeply. "My lady Elizabeth," he said, now looking straight-faced and rather pompous, as though he had not just moments before swept me off my feet.

And the queen, still smiling benignly, called for hippocras to be brought.

As it was the Lenten season, our supper consisted of manchet—fine white bread—and several dishes made of fish. While we ate, the baron described to me the stone castle called Sudeley, three days' journey to the northwest in Gloucestershire.

"It was the pleasure of your brother, the king, to present me with both castle and title," Tom explained. Then, at the queen's urging, Tom Seymour told several tales of wild adventure that I only half believed and made jokes that I did not entirely understand.

So the evening passed merrily, until at last Catherine excused us. The liveried servant reappeared to conduct Kat and me back to our chambers. The fire was dying, and once our maids had removed our gowns and kirtles we retired for warmth to our bed, which turned out to be just as comfortable as it looked.

"What think you now of the baron of Sudeley?" Kat murmured into the darkness.

"I think him——," and here I hesitated, remembering his raucous greeting. "I think him very bold," I replied at last.

"I believe that the baron would have you as his bride," said Kat calmly, as though informing me that a cat likes cream, "were you of an age. And it is not long until you shall be."

"He would marry *me*?" I gasped. "But does not Catherine love him? Does the baron not intend to wed the queen, once her mourning ends?"

"So she hopes. But I believe it is *you* to whom Tom Seymour has lost his heart."

"But, Kat!" I protested, excited but also frightened. "This cannot be! What shall I do?"

"Do nothing at all, dear Elizabeth," Kat replied in that placid way that at times infuriated me. "Wait and see."

Wait and see, I thought as I lay awake, staring into the darkness long after Kat's breathing had deepened in sleep. Too much of my life was "wait and see." Yet, for now, I had no choice—even if I had known what my choices were.

———

NOT LONG AFTER I moved to Catherine's mansion, I learned that Tom's brother, Edward Seymour, had also been given a new title by the king. He was now duke of Somerset. Furthermore, he had been named (or more likely had named himself) lord protector of King Edward.

"This means that Edward Seymour will rule in your brother's stead until the king comes of age," Kat said. "The lord protector is supposed to assist and advise the young king, but you can imagine who will have the real authority for the next nine years."

This was not a surprise, for I had known from the moment my father's death was announced that Edward Seymour intended to grasp the reins of power in England.

One more thing: Tom Seymour had acquired yet another new title. He was now called lord admiral.

I learned this during one of the many dinners and suppers I shared during the following weeks with Queen Catherine. At least half the time, the lord admiral had no navy to command, no ship's crew to attend; he only had us. I was better prepared now for his rambunctious greetings, as he would jump out at me from behind a tapestry or a table, seize me and swing me once or even twice around, and call out, "Welcome, my lady Elizabeth!"

I confess that I was not only prepared for his unconventional greeting, but I now looked forward to it.

Catherine always watched this little ritual with a be-
nevolent smile. When the lord admiral happened to be
away on business, as he often was, I was disappointed.
Of course, I took care to hide my disappointment. It
would not do to have my kind stepmother suspect how
eagerly I awaited those few precious, playful moments
in Tom's arms. I knew from the looks they exchanged
that Catherine was deeply in love with Tom. What was
not so plain was the depth of his feeling for her.

I was, as I have said, thirteen years old at the time,
and I had begun to think of love for myself. Marriage
did not tempt me, although I assumed it was my fate, as
it was the fate of all women. Marriage was about secur-
ing property or power, and seldom had anything to do
with love. I had only to look at my father's six marriages
to shudder at the prospect. Queen Catherine herself
had been married twice to men much older than herself before she married my father, also much older.

Yet, I thought, when I do marry, it must be to a
man like Tom Seymour: handsome, charming, dash-
ing. "And," as Kat was quick to point out, "with a bit of
the devil in him." She made that sound like a *good* thing.
Increasingly, I wasted time in daydreams about what it
might be like to be the wife of the lord admiral.

Then, early one May morning, Queen Catherine
called me to her chambers. I was instructed to come
alone. As soon as I arrived, she dismissed her waiting
women. The queen bade me sit by her side, which I did,

quite mystified by this unusual meeting. "I have a secret for you, Elizabeth, and for you alone. For my sake you must tell no one, although in time all of England will know."

"I swear that I will speak of this to no one," I said breathlessly.

"The lord admiral, baron of Sudeley, and I have married," she said, blushing prettily. "Tom Seymour will no longer be a frequent visitor to our house. He will be living here with us."

My head whirled dizzily with this news. I managed to convey my good wishes, but I confess that I felt a sharp stab of jealousy. Would the raucous greetings and the loud kisses on my cheek come to an end, now that Tom Seymour was my stepmother's husband? It had been foolish of me to dream of him as someday being my own husband, although Kat herself had encouraged that fantasy.

I kept my pledge to the queen and said nothing at all, but finally the baron's presence at odd hours provoked palace gossip. At last the marriage was made public.

Kat Ashley appeared profoundly shocked when she learned of it. "It is much too soon for this," she declared, frowning in disapproval. "The dowager queen is bound to official mourning for a year. King Henry has been dead but three months!"

I did not mention that I had already heard the news

from Catherine's own lips, but I did remind Kat that she herself had predicted this event, as well as the untimely suddenness.

"Do not be pert, miss," Kat admonished me, and I said no more.

THERE WAS ANOTHER change in our living situation, this one more to my liking. With Tom officially part of our Chelsea household, he brought with him his ward, Lady Jane Grey, who was also my cousin—my father's sister Margaret was Jane's grandmother. As young children Jane and I and my brother—and, for a time, Robin Dudley—had shared lessons with our tutors. Jane was nine years old, Edward's elder by only a matter of weeks. Now Jane was under the lord admiral's guardianship, according to an agreement made with her parents.

Jane Grey joined in my studies with my tutor, William Grindal. Despite the difference in our ages, I found Jane entirely my intellectual equal. Her Latin was as fluent as mine, if not better, and she was already reading Greek and Hebrew, in which I had but scant interest. Jane was a brilliant student, and I enjoyed the challenge she provided.

But it appeared that something else was going on. Kat, walking with me in the gardens outside Chelsea Palace, said to me, "I believe the lord admiral intends to see his ward married to the king."

With her small bones and large, solemn eyes, rosy lips, and grave demeanor, Jane seemed a good match for my brother. But there were already rumors that the lord protector had chosen another of our cousins, five-year-old Mary Stuart, Queen of Scots, to become my brother's wife. This struck me as a particularly interesting rivalry—not between the two young girls, who would not be consulted in such a matter, but between the two Seymour brothers. Tom and Edward were each maneuvering to promote his own interests. I had already concluded that Tom's greatest ambition was to replace his brother and become King Edward's lord protector.

My stepmother was caught up in her new marriage. Besides my governess, Kat, Jane was my only friend. She was a sweet-natured girl in addition to having an acute intellect, and we spent many amiable hours in each other's company.

Although I was older by four years, there was little I could teach Jane, with the exception of embroidery. Her keen mind, though, was more challenged by Greek translations than by the couching of gold threads on a piece of silk.

"Oh, dear Elizabeth," she would sigh. "Your stitches are so much finer than mine shall ever be!" And so on. Had she not been my only friend, the only young girl with whom I could speak and walk and ride in the park, I might have found her somewhat annoying at times. She was almost too perfect.

We were sitting at our needlework—I was embellishing the velvet cover of a book as a gift for Catherine, her initials entwined with the lord admiral's, worked in silver wire—when Jane abruptly turned to me and murmured, "I am so happy here, Elizabeth. You cannot imagine how it was."

"I, too, am happy," I responded. *Imagine what?* I wondered.

"I should not speak of it," she said.

"But do, dear cousin," I urged.

"My parents are so severe," she confided in a tearful voice. "Whether I speak or stay silent, sit or stand, eat, drink, be merry or sad, whether I am sewing or playing or dancing or doing anything else, I must do it perfectly. As perfectly as God made the world! If I do not, I am sharply taunted by my mother and cruelly rebuked with pinches and slaps by my father. I sometimes thought myself in hell, until the lord admiral took me as his ward and promised my parents that he would secure a bright future for me."

Jane was not the sort to wail and sob, as some might have done. Instead, after this recital of the terrors of her life with her parents, two perfect tears fell from her eyes, like pearls, and rolled softly down her pale cheeks. And when that was done, she returned to her needlework as though nothing unusual had been said.

"Perhaps it is better to be an orphan," I suggested. "Like me. There is not much that either of us can do with our lives just now, except when others decide to help us." *But someday,* I thought, *it will be different for me. The day will come when I will make my own decisions.* I did not voice my thoughts, for I didn't believe Jane would understand my determination.

"How fortunate for both of us to have the care and affection of the lord admiral," said Jane.

"How fortunate, indeed," I agreed. I wondered if she knew that Tom intended to use her to further his own ambitions.

Many times, I confess it, I simply wanted to be rid of Jane, because I wanted more of Tom Seymour's attention and affection for myself. I knew it was wrong. I knew that Tom was now a married man and that I was betraying my dear stepmother's trust in me.

And yet, how I yearned! I turned his least glance, his smallest joke, into something that meant that he returned my youthful passion. I'm certain that Lady Jane didn't notice the long looks I gave the lord admiral when he barged into our classroom (to the obvious irritation of Professor Grindal) and in his booming voice bade us read aloud to him. Or how, when we supped together, I contrived to sit closer to him.

Kat noticed, though. "For shame, madam!" she admonished me when I had been mooning after him too obviously. "It is apparent to all that you throw yourself in the baron's path at every opportunity. And he the lawful husband of your benefactress!"

But I could not stop myself. Nor did the lord admiral do anything at all to cure me of my lovesickness.

When summer came all of us moved from Chelsea Palace to the countryside of Gloucestershire. The baron of Sudeley had ordered the refurbishment of his castle for his bride, and my lovestruck fantasies continued to bloom there like summer flowers. If Queen Catherine noticed she said nothing, probably assuming I would outgrow my foolishness.

How many times in the months that followed did I wish that she had been right.

CHAPTER 4

Suspicion of Treason

During the weeks and months after my father's death and the accession of my brother to the throne, I heard little from my sister, Mary. She did send me a gift on the occasion of my fourteenth birthday, in September, a pretty pair of kidskin gloves embroidered with pearls. I wrote to thank her, but otherwise I did not write to her at all.

I didn't see her until Christmas, when we were summoned to court by King Edward. Mary arrived adorned in jewels and all sorts of finery, and she looked in better health than she had at our father's funeral. We greeted each other as sisters must, smiling and exchanging pleasantries.

But they were *only* pleasantries. In truth Mary and I had little in common; a difference of seventeen years in age counted for much. Under other circumstances— had she not so hated my mother—Mary might have been a mother to me, as she had been to Edward.

Mary must have been as bewildered as I was by the changes that had taken place in our young brother. Edward at the age of ten was but a slim boy, still a long way from growing into manhood. Yet he appeared determined to live up to his role as our father's son. He behaved as though he already completely filled the shoes of our father!

I ran to embrace him, as I always had. But instead of welcoming me as he once would have, Edward folded his spindly arms across his chest and, frowning, made a sign to his uncle the lord protector.

"My lady Elizabeth," Edward Seymour intoned in that arrogant voice that I so despised, "you are ordered to kneel five times in the king's presence."

Five times! Even our father, who demanded every display of respect from his subjects, had never required that I kneel more than three times! I had learned as a young child never to question the king's will, and so I did now as I was bidden. Only then did King Edward greet me, solemnly holding out his hand so that I might kiss the large ruby ring he wore on his thumb. My brother's behavior seemed ridiculous, even pathetic. *Perhaps,* I thought, *he must act this way in order to feel that he is really and truly the king.*

At each of the nightly Yuletide banquets, my brother sat at the center of the long table with his little dog on his lap. Above him hung the cloth of estate, an elaborate canopy signifying that he—and only he— was the sovereign. Mary and I were led to stools placed far down the table, far enough away from Edward to make certain we weren't in any way covered by that cloth of estate. I wondered if Mary was as irked by this as I was, perhaps even wounded, but she gave no sign, and I decided to make no comment.

It was only when Edward and I were occasionally alone during the visit, when he forgot his posturing and once again called me his Sweet Sister Temperance, his affectionate name for me, that I felt I was with my own dear brother again. Yet the moment Edward Seymour or any of the privy councillors entered the room, Edward immediately became the imperious monarch again, and I was expected to play the role of the obedient subject.

When the season ended, after Twelfth Night, Mary and I left court and went our separate ways without once having spent any time alone together, and I wondered if I had lost my brother forever to the manipulation of his advisers.

IN JANUARY of 1548 London suffered another outbreak of the plague, which carried off my tutor, William Grindal. I mourned him, and then I set about persuading my stepmother that I wished to have the noted scholar Roger Ascham as my tutor in his stead. Catherine had someone else in mind, and so I took my appeal to the lord admiral. I was quite certain of my ability to cajole him, and I knew that Catherine would do whatever Tom decided.

"And do you always get what you want, my lady Elizabeth?" Tom asked in his teasing way.

"Whenever possible, my lord," I said, offering a sweet smile.

"Then you shall have your Master Ascham," he said, patting my arm. And so I did.

I HAD BEEN living under my stepmother's roof for a year when Catherine called me into her chamber one day when Tom was away. She looked tired. I was alarmed to see her lying listlessly on her couch.

"Are you unwell, madam?" I asked.

"I am quite well, Elizabeth," she said, and she smiled wanly. "I am with child." She reached out and grasped my hand in both of hers.

This was another shock to me. I was pleased for her—in her three previous marriages she had borne no children, although those marriages had brought her stepchildren. And now, at last, this. But Catherine was not young. Bearing a child would not be easy for her.

I uttered all the proper words to wish her well, but I'm ashamed to say that I still hadn't banished my yearning for the man who was her husband. More and more I invented excuses to be where he would notice me; I insisted that he must hear me play a new piece upon the virginals or admire a bit of my needlework. My laughter, when Tom was present, pealed a little too loudly.

It is impossible to imagine that Catherine had overlooked my behavior. Kat frowned. More than once even little Jane Grey raised her eyebrows, as though sensing something amiss. At times I feared that someone would write to my sister, Mary, who would censure me or— worse yet—speak to my brother, the king. Edward was becoming unbearably prudish; if he suspected that my heart raced and my hands grew damp in the presence of the lord admiral, what would Edward have said to me? What would he have *done*? He could have sent me to languish far away from Tom and the queen. I shuddered at the trouble in which I could have found myself. Yet I could not stop. Then I did an immensely foolish thing, and it changed everything.

One afternoon Lady Jane and I had labored at our lessons for hours. Professor Ascham prodded us relentlessly as we pored over our books. I had never thought our classroom gloomy before, but suddenly I could bear it no longer. It was late spring, and the weather was warm, sweet, tender. At last we closed our books, laid aside our pens, blotted our papers. While Jane lingered to debate some fine point of Greek grammar with the tutor, I escaped toward the outdoors and the fresh air.

As I rushed through a doorway leading to the stairwell, I collided headlong with the lord admiral. In his usual rambunctious way, Tom caught me in his arms. For a moment we stared at each other. The next moment I found my lips pressed upon his. I did not pull away from the embrace, nor did he.

Then suddenly I heard a shocked voice. "My lord!" Catherine cried. "Elizabeth!"

We drew quickly apart. My stepmother stood on the stairway above us. The lacings of her gown were already stretched tight across her belly, and she looked old and worn. Tom hurried up the stairs to her, protesting, excusing, making a joke. I could not even bear to look at her. I fled to my chambers, my legs trembling and my face hot with shame and embarrassment.

Kat was reading as I rushed in and flung myself miserably upon my bed. "My lady!" Kat exclaimed, dropping her book. "What is it? Are you ill?"

"My stomach pains me." I wept into my pillow. "The monthly curse."

"Let me bring you a potion of herbs," she said.

Obediently I drank the bitter liquid, which did nothing to ease what afflicted me.

That evening I sent word that I was unwell and would not join the others at supper. A servant appeared at my door with a tray. "The dowager queen has sent this for you," she said, and set the tray on my table. But I couldn't bring myself to eat even a morsel.

The next day I received a short note written in Catherine's hand. There was no mention of the scene she had witnessed, only the message that she and the lord admiral would soon leave for Sudeley Castle, where they would await the birth of their child. I was to spend the summer not with them at Sudeley, as I had before, but with Sir Anthony Denny, a gentleman of the privy chamber, and his wife, Joan, at their country house in Cheshunt. I was well acquainted with them, for Lady Joan Denny was Kat's sister.

I look forward to happy reports from you of a pleasant summer, Catherine wrote.

I am forever grateful to the queen. She sent me away not only to preserve her marriage but to preserve my reputation, which could have been permanently damaged if I had remained any longer in the presence of Tom Seymour.

Still deeply ashamed of what had happened, I presented myself on the day after Whitsunday in the queen's chambers to make my farewells. "Oh, Your Majesty," I stammered, but my words were halted by a rush of tears.

"It is all right, Elizabeth," she said kindly, and wiped my tears with her own handkerchief. "I understand. Truly I do. Now go." And she pushed me gently away.

Catherine and I exchanged letters throughout the summer. For the most part my life became a scholarly one, which suited me well, for it occupied my mind. Most of the day was spent with Mr. Ascham, reading the New Testament in Greek and translating the works of Cicero and Livy from Latin to English and then back into Latin again.

I did miss Jane Grey, who was at Sudeley Castle with Catherine and Tom. But I had Kat, and her sister Lady Joan was a jolly sort who never let on that she knew the cause of my exile, although she had certainly heard of it from Kat.

AT THE BEGINNING of September, we received joyous news at Cheshunt from Tom Seymour of the birth of a healthy infant daughter, to be named Mary. But only days later my joy turned to sorrow when a messenger brought news of Catherine's death. My grief at her loss was compounded by the guilt I felt. Had I somehow contributed to her death by my actions? Then I heard that Jane Grey had taken the role of chief mourner at her funeral. I knew that I had forfeited that privilege with my heedless behavior. Lady Jane was far more virtuous than I and deserved the role.

GRIEF CONSUMED ME. I wept, slept little, ate next to nothing. Queen Catherine had been my champion, my supporter. What would happen to me now that she was gone? Perhaps, I dared to hope, Tom would come to my rescue. How naive I was still! Soon after my fifteenth birthday, I returned with my household to Hatfield Palace and waited.

"You watch," Kat whispered one night behind our bed curtains. "Tom Seymour will come courting you as soon as he decently can." It was as though Kat could read my most secret thoughts and desires. "He intends to have you as his wife after all. He has even kept on all of the queen's servants. Lady Jane has returned to her parents' home. Why else would he need a household of two hundred, save for a princess bride?"

"I cannot imagine," I murmured, unwilling to confess even to Kat that I had entertained this notion.

"You do not want to be like your sister, Mary, now, do you, growing old alone?" Kat persisted.

I did not. But I didn't know then how much my world had changed.

I received no Yuletide invitation to court from my brother, and that troubled me. Had he heard about the reason for my stay at Cheshunt? Had Tom admitted something? I feared that Edward was punishing me by banishing me from court, and several times I tried to write to him. But I could not think what to say, and each effort ended in pieces of parchment torn up and flung away.

One morning in January of 1549, as I prepared to go to chapel, I heard Kat scream. I ran down the staircase and saw Kat and Mr. Parry, my cofferer, surrounded by guards in the king's livery. The guards had dragged them out of the palace.

I rushed toward Kat, but Sir Robert Tyrwhitt, a member of the privy council, blocked my way. "Lady Elizabeth," he said, bowing respectfully.

"Where are you taking them?" I cried.

"To the Tower of London."

"But why? By whose order?"

"For questioning, by order of His Majesty, King Edward," said Sir Robert.

I ran after the guards and tried to fling myself upon Kat. One of the guards seized and held me roughly. I was forced to watch helplessly as the prisoners were taken away. Kat was wailing, Mr. Parry repeating, "I am innocent, I am innocent."

When they had gone Sir Robert turned his attention to me, as I stood alone and trembling. Eyebrows wild as brambles gave him a fearsome look. "The lord admiral, baron of Sudeley, has been arrested," he said gravely. "And the members of the privy council have a number of questions for you, madam."

"Arrested! But why?" I collapsed onto a nearby bench, my mind racing: *What has he done? Why am I to be questioned?* Then, as calmly as I could manage, I asked, "I beg you, Sir Robert, tell me what has happened."

In somber tones Sir Robert described the events leading up to Tom Seymour's arrest. "The lord admiral went late one night to the king's bedchamber, planning to kidnap him. When the king's little dog began to bark, the lord admiral shot and killed the dog. The guards discovered the lord admiral and seized him."

"My God!" I cried. "What are the charges against him?"

"There are many, all treasonous," Sir Robert informed me. "The gravest charge is his attempt to kidnap the king. But it seems that the baron was scheming to marry you, Lady Elizabeth, without seeking the permission of the king, the privy council, or the lord protector."

"To marry *me*?" I felt faint. "But there is no truth to this allegation!"

Sir Robert continued as though I had not spoken. "To marry an heir to the throne without the king's permission is an act of treason, punishable by death. It was believed that Mistress Ashley and Mr. Parry knew of Baron Sudeley's plan and agreed to help him."

I was stunned. Sir Robert escorted me to my chambers, but before I could gather my wits, his interrogation began. *Did Mr. Parry and Mistress Ashley plot to marry you to the lord admiral? No? Are you quite certain? Think carefully. There was a plot, was there not? Please do not lie, madam. The truth will be found out.*

Over and over Sir Robert, eyes fierce as a hawk's, insisted that I knew more than I was admitting. And I did! I could not forget all those midnight conversations with Kat: *He intends to have you as his wife after all.* But those were not a plot—only speculation, without any substance! I knew that I must show no weakness, confess nothing, not even the most innocent conversation. If necessary, I must lie, and lie well.

Everything depended upon my convincing replies. Over and over I denied the accusations, all the while beside myself with worry about what might be happening to Kat and Mr. Parry in the Tower and what confessions might be wrung from them by torture or threats of it.

Then Sir Robert moved himself into my palace. Day after day, week upon week, the questioning went on. There was no escape from it. He was pitiless, waiting for me to emerge from my bedchamber, pounding on my door if I did not appear early enough to suit him. And there was no respite at night, either, no loving Kat to soothe my frayed nerves. I was fifteen, and I had absolutely no one to help me.

At first I wept my protest. My tears had no effect; Sir Robert simply repeated the questions. Then I kept silent, refusing to answer. At times I offered reasonable replies, but this didn't appease him. Tyrwhitt did not believe me, that was plain, but he could prove nothing.

I had questions of my own: *Had Tom planned to marry me? What was he doing outside Edward's bedchamber? Had he really intended to kidnap the king? For what purpose?* I dared not ask any of them, but slowly, as I continued to think, it became clear to me that Tom's interest in me had been solely for his own advancement. This angered me. For this man I had betrayed my stepmother's generous kindness, and he had in turn only wanted to use me.

After I had endured several weeks of relentless interrogation, Sir Robert's wife arrived and announced that she would take Kat's place as my governess. I was acquainted with Lady Tyrwhitt, one of Queen Catherine's stepdaughters by a previous marriage, and I knew her to be small-minded and peevish. I wept endless tears at this change. I could neither eat nor sleep. I wanted Kat! I would have Kat or no one! To be truthful it was far harder on me to lose Kat Ashley, my faithful companion of the past dozen years, than it had been to lose others, who were my kin. Kat was like both mother and father to me.

Sir Robert and his stony-faced wife were not moved by my tears. Desperate, I wrote to the lord protector, Edward Seymour, pleading my innocence in all things as well as the innocence of my friends, and begging that Kat be sent back to me. But the lord protector only replied that I must confess to a plot! I refused, swearing again that there *was* no plot.

Lady Tyrwhitt stayed on, her face permanently creased in a disapproving frown. My new governess and I found little ways to torment each other. I insisted that I must have the bed curtains open and all the candles burning throughout the night, saying that I couldn't sleep without them. This wasn't the case, but I had discovered that the light disturbed her.

She, for her part, refused to let me ride my horse or walk with my ladies-in-waiting unless either she or Sir Robert accompanied us. She was an imperious nag with a whining voice. I didn't know how Sir Robert could abide her.

It was Lady Tyrwhitt who brought me the news while I sat at my needlework: "The lord admiral has been sentenced to die for treason," she announced, relishing her duty, for she plainly despised him. "And if your friends are not mindful, they will share his fate."

I knew that she said this to frighten me. I took care

not to show my fear—which was very real—and scarcely missed a stitch. My fear was not for Tom Seymour. I had stopped loving Tom when I understood how little I meant to him. Lately there were even rumors, that he had caused Queen Catherine's death by poison, although I didn't believe he had. And what of my poor brother? How betrayed and frightened *he* must have felt by this uncle he had loved.

But it was for Mr. Parry and Kat that I truly feared. They had done nothing. At times I paused to wonder what had become of Catherine's baby daughter, who'd gone to the care of Tom's mother. Was the little girl still alive? Would she grow up to hear tales of her father's execution, as I had of my mother's?

Before being led to his beheading on Tower Hill, on the twentieth of March, 1549, Tom Seymour once again assured the privy council of my innocence. Apparently they believed him—or else had given up the attempt to wring a confession from me. Without explanation or apology, the Tyrwhitts departed from Hatfield, and soon thereafter Mr. Parry and Kat Ashley returned to my household.

I had servants posted along the road to alert me of their approach, and I rode out to meet them. As I embraced them both I said, "Tonight we shall celebrate with a fine feast. Tomorrow you shall tell me your stories."

THE STRUGGLE for power continued. The next man to be arrested and imprisoned in the Tower was Edward

Seymour himself, defeated as lord protector by his rival, John Dudley, father of my old friend Robin. Fond as I had always been of Robin, I did not like his father, who could not be trusted to keep his word. In my opinion John Dudley was no better than Edward Seymour, and perhaps even worse, and now Dudley was the lord protector of King Edward.

I was far more cautious than I had been two years earlier, when my head was filled with the attentions of Tom Seymour. I had learned early that I must be very careful of what I say, what I do, with whom I associate. Next I had learned to lie cleverly to protect myself, if I must. My father's court had been a dangerous place filled with intrigue. But my father, the king, had kept the reins of power firmly in his grasp. Young King Edward was a different story. His power was a sham: Forcing his subjects to kneel five times in his presence was no power at all.

Now I learned to wait. I knew that I had the strength to do so.

CHAPTER 5

King Edward's Court

My banishment ended at Yuletide in the year 1549, when Edward once again invited me to court. I had been absent for eighteen months, and in that time I had grown up. At sixteen I was no longer a silly young girl who could be taken in by the wiles of a handsome older man. By the use of my wits, I had managed to survive Sir Robert Tyrwhitt's grueling interrogation, although rumors of my involvement with Tom Seymour had been court gossip for many weeks. Part of my inheritance from my father had finally come into my hands, and I could afford to live as I pleased.

I was well aware of my looks. I had reached my full height, taller than my sister by nearly a hand span, and I was slender and fashionably small breasted. My hair was a striking golden red, long and thick, curling and spiraling around my face and loose upon my shoulders. My eyes were dark, my skin pale as alabaster. Studying myself in the mirror, I knew that no man would look at me with disinterest.

I intended to make my return to court a triumph. Mary had long been a great favorite, while in the past I had been generally ignored, and I was determined to be the almost forgotten princess no longer. Mary would come decked in jewels; therefore, I would wear only a jeweled ring or two, to show off my hands, which I thought my best feature. Mary would dress in the bright colors and rich fabrics she favored; I would appear in simple black or white gowns, ordered from France. I was young; Mary was not, and all her silks and jewels could not disguise that. I was not just her sister, Elizabeth—I was the proud daughter of King Henry VIII, and I wanted everyone to be aware of it.

A royal escort of a hundred liveried horsemen accompanied me to London on the week before Christmas. If people had thought ill of me because of gossip surrounding Tom Seymour, it now seemed forgotten. I could feel all eyes upon me when I arrived at St. James's Palace and made my way to the king's presence chamber. Ladies and gentlemen of the court outdid themselves with bows and curtsies, smiles and greetings.

"Sweet Sister Temperance!" King Edward called out after I had gone through the courtesies he demanded—

one, two, three, four, five. That much had not changed! Then he rose and held out his ring, and I kissed it.

But there was no sign of Mary.

"I invited her," my brother said. "I wrote to her in my own hand and asked her to join us. She replied that her health is poor, but that she will come to visit for a few days in the new year."

I thought her absence odd. "Mary has excused herself from the Yuletide celebrations," I told Kat as my maids dressed me for the evening's banquet.

"Mary fears she would not be allowed to hear the Roman Mass at Christmas if she came to court," Kat said, assuring me that she had this knowledge on good authority.

Acts of Parliament during my father's reign had outlawed the Roman Catholic Church in England. Edward and I had been raised as Protestants, and Edward was now head of the Church of England, the one true church. Despite all, Mary persisted in her practice of Catholicism, the faith of her mother and of her childhood.

For the next three weeks, my brother and I spent many hours in each other's company, walking, talking, playing quiet games of chess. During this time we were nearly as close and comfortable with each other as we had been as children. But each night a royal banquet was held in the Great Hall for at least a hundred guests, and then Edward was transformed again into a strutting, posturing monarch. I found such behavior revolting, but it was forbidden to criticize the king. As always I was seated at some distance from Edward.

Although he appeared to eat very little at the nightly feasts, my brother ordered two courses to be served, each course consisting of at least two dozen dishes—roast pig, frumenty with venison, all kinds of fish and fowl, pasties and puddings—each presented, tasted, and then carried off.

For the Christmas feast itself, trumpet fanfares announced the arrival of the boar's head, carried in on a golden charger, its tusks gilded and set aflame. The entire company sang an old carol while the servants knelt and presented the boar's head to the king.

Yuletide climaxed with Twelfth Night, more festive and riotous than all the feasts that had preceded it. The main event was the choosing of the Lord of Misrule. In my father's time the singing and dancing that followed had continued until dawn. Since my brother had come to the throne, the dancing was much more restrained and ended at an earlier hour. Still, I enjoyed what dancing was permitted and had no lack of partners.

Suddenly Robin Dudley appeared before me. I had not seen him since I was last at court. Now, at sixteen, he had grown much taller and was exceedingly well made. My brother had appointed him Master of the Buckhounds. Edward loved to hunt deer in the company of Robin and his hounds, and Robin, I had heard,

was now much at court. I was overjoyed to see him
again.

"I must speak to you in private, Elizabeth," he whispered as the music began and we briefly joined hands to
execute certain steps.

This provoked my curiosity, but I could only smile
as we whirled apart. I thought quickly. *Where can we meet
without being interrupted?* On this night I knew of one place
almost certain to be deserted. "The chapel royal," I
murmured as again our hands joined. "When the next
dance begins."

It was easy enough to slip away, and I waited impatiently in the empty chapel royal. What would Robin
have to say? Was it something about King Edward? Something about me?

Moments later Robin appeared in the shadows.
Then he stepped into the flickering light of the few
candles that had been left burning.

"Elizabeth," he said, and I noted that his voice was
husky. Without waiting for my response, he hurried on.
"I am betrothed."

"Oh? To what fortunate lady?" I asked. I confess that
the news took me unawares.

"Amy Robsart. We are to be married in June."

"Married in June!" I exclaimed.

That the wealthy Robsarts and the ambitious Dudleys saw a betrothal as a mutual advantage was no surprise. Betrothals are pledges that bind two people for a

year, but often the betrothals are broken, or the year allowed to pass with neither a marriage nor a renewal of the pledge. That a wedding date had actually been set did indeed astonish me. I suppose I somehow hoped that my old friend would remain free. My feelings made no sense, and I kept silent, not trusting my voice to conceal them.

"Would that it were you, Elizabeth!" he cried, and for one wild moment I wanted to throw myself into his arms.

But I did nothing of the sort. "I shall never marry, Robin," I said. "Not you, nor anyone."

I turned away and hurried out of the chapel. What had I said? *I shall never marry.* Did I truly mean it? *Never?* I felt confused, almost giddy. But in minutes I was following the complicated steps of a gigue with Guildford Dudley, Robin's younger, clumsier, and far less comely brother.

For the next four days, I had no further conversations with Robin. I felt that he was avoiding me, and I did not go out of my way to seek his company. But my own words continued to echo in my head: *I shall never marry.* I felt as though I had somehow crossed a vast ocean, never to return.

DAYS LATER I bade my brother farewell. My visit to court had been a success, but still it was with relief that I headed north for Hatfield with my retinue. My only regular visitor during the dark, cold days of winter was

Sir William Cecil, a member of my brother's privy council and the only one of the sixteen men whom I believed to be above reproach. To this sober and honest gentleman, I had entrusted the management of my financial affairs.

I was not unhappy during this quiet time, although I do confess to bouts of restlessness. To cure them I often called for one of my geldings to be saddled and brought to me. "I fear that you will break your neck!" Kat invariably fretted, wringing her hands. But I always returned muddy, wet, and bedraggled from the hard, fast ride over the heath, unharmed and thoroughly exhilarated. I loved the danger, and on the back of a horse I felt as though I was in charge of my life.

I did occasionally think of Robin, but I had made up my mind that no man should be my undoing, as Tom Seymour nearly had been.

WINTER WAS reluctantly yielding to spring when I was again summoned to visit my brother, during Passiontide in 1550. The court had moved to Hampton Court, a sumptuous palace on the Thames several miles upriver from London. There were no festive banquets in that penitential season, only plain Lenten fare during the two weeks before the Great Feast of Easter.

At twelve Edward was thin and frail-looking, one shoulder held higher than the other. He was shortsighted, and he squinted in order to see objects at a distance. In an attempt to mimic our strong, athletic father, he swaggered about with his small fists planted on his narrow hips and his delicate features twisted in a scowl. And even when we dined in private, his carvers and cupbearers were ordered to doff their caps and drop to their knees to serve him. He tried to utter thunderous oaths, but his voice wobbled and squeaked between boy's and man's.

It had become a kind of game with Edward to elude the prying eyes of John Dudley, who now bore the title of duke of Northumberland. Dudley and the other privy councillors watched the king like falcons about to swoop down on a hapless rabbit. To escape their vigilant gaze, my brother and I hurried off to the maze of hedges that our father had ordered built in the gardens at Hampton Court. Edward had memorized every twist and turn among the tall privets, and once we'd found the heart of the maze, we believed we had a little time in which to speak privately before anyone discovered us.

Wrapped in furs against the damp, chill wind that swept off the river, Edward settled himself on a stone bench to rest and gestured for me to kneel upon the cold ground. Even under these circumstances he would not share the bench with me. I wanted to shout at him, "Edward, I am your sister! There is no cloth of estate here!" But I did not. No matter how foolish the boy's behavior, I was the king's subject and dared not correct him or point out his follies. And so I dutifully bit my tongue to silence and shivered on my knees.

"Sweet Sister Temperance," Edward began, as he usually did when he addressed me, "I worry myself about our sister."

"Mary? What is wrong, my lord? Is she not coming here to join us for Easter?"

"She is not. Again she has refused, making some excuse. She hints that she suspects a plot against her."

"Surely she is mistaken, my lord," I said, but I was thinking, *Doubtless she is* not *mistaken.* I did not trust the king's advisers, especially Dudley, and probably, quite rightly, Mary didn't either.

Edward sighed. "She refuses to give up her devotion to the Catholic Church. But she must! Word has reached the councillors that not only does she continue to hear Mass daily but that her entire household joins her. And this has been strictly forbidden! Why do you suppose she clings to these practices so stubbornly? It would be so much easier to agree to what the law demands."

"I care deeply for our sister," I answered carefully, as custom required, "but I neither understand nor approve of her religious ideas. Could she not learn to praise God as a Protestant?"

Edward suffered a fit of coughing. When it had passed he said, "I have been told that Mary may try to flee the country. She has been in contact with the Emperor Charles. She asked him to send a ship to take her away to Flanders."

Emperor Charles was Mary's cousin on her mother's side. And he was the most powerful man in Europe. But for him to do as Mary asked was risky. Suppose Mary were to marry a Catholic king who might attempt to overthrow Edward and restore Catholicism? The emperor would feel obliged to fight for Mary, and he'd find himself at war against England.

"But why would she want to run away?" I asked.

Edward was silent for a time, and we both listened for the footsteps of those who'd surely have been sent to find us. "Because she believes I would have her put to death. Dear Elizabeth, I should so hate to do that! She is like a mother to me, and I do love her so!"

I was shocked. This was the first I had heard him speak of such a thing. Put Mary to death? Would he really do that—execute his own sister? He looked so upset that I was also fairly certain it was not his idea. "But why? What has she done to deserve death? And on whose advice would you have our sister executed?" I asked.

"The councillors have spoken of it," Edward said, weeping now. "Because she will not obey the laws and give up her foolish religion! They discuss it among themselves, and it upsets me terribly that they do so. But I must do as they say, especially Dudley, for he knows what is best for England and I do not!"

I could say nothing. To contradict him, even in private, was very dangerous. My brother was highly intelligent, but he was still only a boy. With the exception of Cecil, the privy councillors hovered over him and dictated his every move, always for their own benefit. "The king lacks the strength of his own will," Kat had often said. "Dudley has made him a doll-puppet."

Now, before we could say more, we heard voices. They were coming closer. I squeezed Edward's hand, and like naughty children we waited to be found.

HATFIELD, which now belonged to me, had been cleansed in my absence. The soiled rush mats on the floors had been removed and sweet-smelling ones laid in their place. Wall hangings and tapestries blackened with soot from the winter fires had been taken down and exposed to fresh air, the walls scrubbed and whitened. Bed hangings and coverlets and mattresses stuffed with wool were refreshed, mended, replaced. Silver and gold plate was polished, linens bleached in the sunshine. I found everything in good order.

I had the responsibility of overseeing a great estate that produced quantities of mutton and beef, wool and leather, as well as fat for making candles and soap. Much of the production of Hatfield went to supply King Edward's court. It was my pleasure to ride out to watch the peasants at their labors. As long as I lived a quiet country life, away from the intrigue of court, I felt that I was in no danger.

Then came an invitation to attend the wedding of

Robin Dudley to Amy Robsart. I had grown accustomed to the idea that my old friend would soon be a married man.

On a fine, sunny day in June, I traveled from Hatfield with a large retinue to Windsor Castle. My brother, who had come from London with a much larger retinue, was given the place of honor at the wedding, and I a place lower down. Among the guests was Lady Jane Grey, now so delicately beautiful and so elegantly gowned that she risked drawing undue attention away from the bride.

I was happy to see Jane, and we contrived to have a few moments to talk together. "My life is a misery," she confided at once. "I do believe that God intends for me to suffer."

"I do not believe that God intends for any of His creatures to suffer," I said, but before I could determine the cause of her misery, we were separated by a band of musicians. I suspected that she was getting on with her cruel parents no better than she ever had.

Amy Robsart was a plump little thing, nearly swallowed up in an overwrought gown of silver tissue. Two young boys led her to the church, carrying branches of rosemary, gilded and swagged with silk ribbons. They were accompanied by a dozen maidens, each bearing a bride cake. Musicians piped a merry tune. But my eye was drawn to Robin, who, looking as fine as I have ever seen him, arrived at the church doors with his gentlemen.

Robin and his bride exchanged their vows, and once the wedding ring had been placed upon fair Amy's thumb, the priest covered them with the nuptial veil and blessed the marriage. That done, we all made our way to the castle along a path strewn with rose petals and rosemary.

We feasted and danced quite decorously, and so the day passed. I have always enjoyed weddings, but I confess that about this one I felt differently. Did Robin Dudley truly love Amy? I doubted it. Love has nothing to do with marriage, but money does. Amy had indeed made her husband quite rich. There was no reason I should have suffered such pangs of the heart. Yet it was as though a door I'd not noticed before had been suddenly and forever shut.

CHAPTER 6

The Dying King

*J*ust after my seventeenth birthday, in September, a messenger arrived at Hatfield with a letter from Robin's father, John Dudley, the lord protector. I broke the seal and read the brief message: *It is the king's opinion that the time has come for you to wed,* he wrote, adding that in his position as head of the privy council, he was considering several possible suitors. *It shall be my duty to inform you as negotiations proceed.* The letter ended with all sorts of wishes for my good health and was decorated with ornamental flourishes.

I was furious. "Kat!" I called out so loudly that my voice echoed through the palace. "Kat, where are you? I need you at once!"

Moments later Kat rushed in, her cap askew. "My lady Elizabeth! What is it?"

I was so angry I could hardly speak. I thrust the offensive letter into Kat's hands. "Read this!" I commanded.

Kat did so and then glanced up at me with her mild blue eyes. "Why does this upset you so, Elizabeth?" she asked. "You are of an age. It is not unexpected, surely?"

"Kat, is it possible that you do not understand? Have you not heard me speak of this in the past?" I demanded hotly. "*I do not wish to marry!*"

Kat studied me carefully. "Come," she said at last, "let us have some ale, and we can discuss the matter."

"There is nothing to discuss," I declared when two silver tankards of ale had been brought to us. "I have thought it over quite carefully for some time, and my mind is made up. I shall not change it. *I shall not marry.*"

"But you must, Elizabeth!" Kat insisted. "It is not possible for you *not* to marry! Firstly, it is expected of you, as it is of every woman. Secondly, to remain unmarried would be unwise for your health, both in body and in mind. Just look at your poor sister!"

"That is my sister's matter, and this is mine," I snapped. "I intend to remain a virgin."

I thought I detected a slight smile on Kat's lips. "Is it not imaginable," she asked, "that you might change your mind in the future? If the right man should happen along?"

"Never!" I said, setting down my tankard of ale so

hard that the amber liquid splashed upon my gown. "Never!"

Wisely, Kat said no more, and I scribbled a brief note to the lord protector. "I do not wish to marry," I wrote. Having nothing more to add, I dated it and signed my name. Then I summoned the messenger to carry my letter back to London.

In the months that followed, I learned that John Dudley had ignored my letter and my wishes. He had entered into negotiations with four foreign noblemen—one was a Frenchman, one a German, and two were Italians, all with fathers or brothers who were powerful dukes.

As soon as I heard of it, I swore that I would accept none of them, nor any other. For the time being at least, God's grace shone upon me. In all four instances the negotiations came to nothing. I did understand, though, that the demand that I marry sooner rather than later would be unrelenting.

AS SEASON followed season I divided my life between quiet times in the country with my former tutor, Professor Ascham, as my intellectual companion, and lively visits to court, where I was much in my brother's favor. I enjoyed the attention I received as the king's sister. Although Edward still insisted upon his rituals, I did love my brother dearly and cherished my time with him. But I also pitied him.

"You have no idea how terrible it is, dear sister,"

Edward once confided when we had again managed to elude the advisers who seemed always to surround him.

"Terrible how?" I asked.

"My uncle Edward Seymour has been let out of the Tower and once again serves on the council. He and Dudley argue and shout at each other, and no one listens to me! I want so much to be a good king, and I know that I can do it, if they will only let me. But they will allow me to do nothing at all." And he fell weeping into my arms.

IN THE SUMMER of 1551, the sweating sickness scourged England as it had not done for many years. Visitors to Hatfield Palace told me that in London the church bells tolled ceaselessly for the dead. Away from the ill humors of the city, I prayed that we might be spared. I was especially worried about Edward.

Thanks be to God he escaped the sweat, as did I and others close to me. But many were not so fortunate; in all, fifty thousand people died that summer.

Although Edward did not fall victim to the sweat, I could see that my brother's health was in alarming decline. When I attended court at Christmas 1551, my fourteen-year-old brother looked more frail than ever.

Another year passed, during which Dudley succeeded in permanently removing his chief rival, Edward Seymour, by ordering his execution. It must have been a terrible time for my brother, who once again had to sign the order for an uncle's death.

I attended court when King Edward summoned me, always dreading that first sight of him and the obvious signs of declining strength. I saw Mary not at all during this time. In the winter of 1553, I translated from Italian a sermon by a religious reformer whose work had impressed me deeply. I copied this translation onto parchment in my most elegant handwriting and sent it to Edward. *No one can match the extent of my love and good feeling toward you,* I wrote to him with great sincerity.

In his letter of thanks, I saw in both his words and his wavering script that my brother was very ill. I sent a message at once that I was coming to visit him.

The early spring weather did not favor my journey from Hatfield to London, and my retinue and I found ourselves pelted with stinging sleet. As we neared our destination, we were met by a group of sodden and mud-splattered men who signaled us to halt. One of the men, whom I recognized as a member of the privy council, presented me with a letter ordering me to turn back.

At first I thought to ignore the letter, signed not by King Edward but by John Dudley, duke of Northumberland.

"The king is my brother," I said, addressing the councillor, "and I shall see him unless he himself turns me away."

"My lady Elizabeth," he replied, "I assure you that you will be refused admission to the king's bedchamber."

For a long moment the councillor and I stared at each other. But my will was no match for John Dudley's.

I had no doubt that if I continued on, Dudley would find a pretext to have me seized and imprisoned—or worse. Angrily I turned my horse back toward Hatfield.

My anger was quickly replaced by sadness; my brother was dying. But in the midst of my sorrow came the growing realization that, according to the order of succession established by our father's will, Mary would become queen at Edward's death. And that day was not far away. My mind leaped to the future: Edward had not lived long enough to produce an heir. Mary, at thirty-three, was still unmarried. Instead of standing far from the throne, I would soon be next in line. That realization thrilled me, but it also frightened me. I was beginning to understand that many people, beginning with John Dudley and the privy councillors, would stop at nothing—including murder—to block Mary's way, and then mine.

And so, in the days that followed, I prayed fervently for my brother and, in a state of high anxiety, awaited further word. My own physician kept me informed: Edward was coughing blood, his body wasting away, his mind fevered and disturbed. The end was near.

BECAUSE I SPENT most of my time at Hatfield, the gossip of the court was always stale and often somewhat altered by the time it reached me. Thus I was unprepared for the announcement, in May, of the betrothal of Jane Grey to John Dudley's youngest son, Robin's brother Guildford.

Several of my ladies-in-waiting devoured gossip as a thirsty horse drinks water; they were also well connected, with brothers and cousins at court. These ladies—Cynthia, Marian, and Letitia—enjoyed bringing me morsels of rumor and scandal, which they presented as we sat at our needlework. Petty gossip to them was to me a matter of life and death, but I pretended to delight in their revelations.

"Lady Jane does not want this marriage, not at all," reported Lady Cynthia, an auburn-haired young woman with emerald green eyes.

"Why not?"

"She claims that she is already promised to Edward Seymour's son, Lord Hertford."

"Lord Hertford!" I exclaimed. "She prefers marriage to a spindleshanks like Hertford to Guildford Dudley?"

"Guildford is not ill favored," Lady Letitia granted, "although not nearly so handsome as his brother Robin." She shot me a mischievous glance, which I blandly ignored. "But Jane cannot abide John Dudley or his wife. The duchess has Guildford completely under her thumb, I hear."

"Perhaps Lady Jane will find a way out," I suggested. I regretted now that Jane and I were not as close as we once had been, and I wished that she had confided in me.

"The wedding is to take place in a fortnight," said Lady Marian, a plain and practical sort. "There is so little time that she is not even to have a new gown.

John Dudley has given them access to the royal wardrobe and told them to help themselves to whatever finery they choose."

"But," said Cynthia, knotting her silken thread with a flourish, "Lady Jane was assured by her parents that her life will go on as before, and she shall continue to live at home, as she has since the death of the dowager queen. They have promised that her studies will proceed uninterrupted."

"Dear Jane!" I exclaimed. "Being able to pursue her studies will be of utmost importance to her." *So it's to be a marriage in name only, until an heir is wanted,* I thought. *What will be the next twist in this plot?*

Jane and her family were always in evidence at court events—they were our cousins. Jane's mother, Frances, was my father's niece. Jane was the eldest of three daughters; there were no sons. According to my father's will, Frances Grey stood in the line of succession after Mary and me; she was then followed in turn by Jane and Jane's two younger sisters.

It was an unusual state of affairs that there were no males in line for the crown. But this could be remedied by the right marriage. A husband would naturally rule in his wife's stead until a male heir was born. And so it became clear to me that John Dudley's plan was to marry his son to Jane, who was now fourth in line for the throne. Would his next step be to eliminate those in line ahead of Jane—Mary and me? I saw that John Dudley was even more dangerous than I'd imagined.

Within hours of receiving this information, I sent for William Cecil, on the pretext of needing his opinion on the purchase of a property bordering my estate. The messenger returned with the information that Cecil was suffering from a fever but would call upon me when he recovered.

I would have to survive in the meantime on crumbs of gossip. Poor Kat bore the brunt of my impatience. Once I even snatched a bit of needlework from her hands and ripped out some of the stitches. "Do them over!" I cried, thrusting the piece back at her and storming out of the chamber.

I WAS NOT invited to the wedding. It was an insult, of course, but John Dudley was plainly so certain of his power that he didn't care *whom* he insulted. I counted for nothing. This slight served only to feed my suspicions, fuel my anger, and strengthen my resolve that one day all of England would recognize my importance.

Lady Marian's sister-in-law sent us word of it all. "Jane was gowned in cloth of gold with a cloak of silver tissue," Marian said. "And her hair was combed and plaited and hung down her back in a way that many thought quite odd. Her headdress was green velvet covered all over with precious stones."

Jane was not the only bride at the wedding, I learned; she was but one of three that day. All in one fell swoop, John Dudley married his daughter, Catherine, to another councillor, and Jane's sister, who was also named Catherine, was married to the son of a third councillor. What a knot of conspirators John Dudley had contrived! I thought I would go mad if I did not soon have Cecil's explanation of it all.

Marian continued her tale. "When the feasting was done, the three bridegrooms departed for the royal tilt-yard at Whitehall for a friendly joust."

"The brides no doubt stayed behind and silently rejoiced at being left to themselves for a while longer," I suggested. But perhaps I was simply speaking for myself.

CECIL FINALLY arrived at Hatfield in June, apparently fully recovered and dressed, as always, in somber black with the smallest of neck ruffs. I called for my gelding, and we set off to inspect the neighboring property. I wasted no time in bringing up my worries.

"As you must know, I am most interested in the marriage of my cousin Jane to Guildford Dudley."

"As well you might be, for some of it concerns you, madam."

"Then tell me."

"After the wedding Jane returned to her parents' home, as she had been promised. But that promise was broken ten days later when she was taken to live with Guildford at the Dudleys' home. John Dudley informed the Greys of his plan for his new daughter-in-law: King Edward, aware that he was dying, wished to make changes in the succession. He had written out a document called *The Device for the Succession.* Your sister, Mary, was struck from the line of succession. And I am sorry to say that your name has also been stricken. Jane's mother has relinquished her claim, in favor of her daughter. At Edward's death Lady Jane Dudley, as she is now called, will be crowned queen."

"But he cannot do that!" I shouted, reining in my horse sharply. "This violates my father's will!"

Cecil also stopped his horse, and we sat facing each other. "But he *has* done it, my lady. Your brother, the king, is very weak. John Dudley has total power over him."

"When did you learn of this?" I demanded.

"After the fact, madam. Just days ago Dudley gathered the privy council together in the king's presence chamber. These were his words, as nearly as I can recall:

" 'In order to be faithful to his father's name and wishes and to fulfill his duty to God, King Edward has decided that the crown must not pass to his sister Mary, who breaks the king's law and violates her father's memory with her persistence in the Catholic faith.' "

"But what about *me*?" I shrieked. "I am not a Catholic! My brother could not have accused me of violating the faith, for I am as Protestant as the king! He cannot simply eliminate me!"

"Dudley claims that the king was equally insistent that the crown not go to 'the lady Elizabeth.' He feels that it would cause disharmony to eliminate one sister and not the other. Or so Dudley claims."

Dudley's plan was now apparent to all. At his instruction the new queen, Jane, would name Guildford
as the new king. Guildford would do as his father told
him, and John Dudley, duke of Northumberland, would
hold the real power in the kingdom.

I had by then completely lost my temper. I leaped
from my horse, snatched up a handful of stones that
were lying about, and threw them as hard as I could at a
fence post nearby. The fence post was a poor substitute
for John Dudley, and the stones bounced off harmlessly.
Cecil watched me in silence. My three ladies, who had
been riding decorously some distance behind us, drew
up their mounts and stared. When I had no more stones,
I flung clods of dirt. My headdress flew off, my gown was
streaked with dirt, and my hair came undone.

"But it is not completely settled yet, is it?" I asked,
still breathless but calmer now that my temper had at
last worn itself out. "Surely Parliament must approve
Edward's *Device for the Succession.* If the privy council
chooses, the device can be declared illegal, can it not?"

Cecil dismounted and helped me back onto my
horse. "You are right, madam," he sighed. "But you
were not present with the councillors to hear Dudley's
arguments and threats. He pounded the table, and in
his thundering voice he issued this warning: 'If Mary as-
cends to the throne, every man among us will be punished for disloyalty. Every man among us will be sent to
the Tower, and every man among us will have his head
on the block.'"

At that moment a dark cloud passed over the sun, and I shivered. "And what was the conclusion of the council?" I asked with a sick feeling, certain I already knew the answer.

"A vote was taken. There was but one dissenting vote—mine. Every man but one agreed that Lady Jane Dudley will be the next queen."

CHAPTER 7

Two Queens

Poor Jane! She was a brilliant scholar, but she was completely innocent in the ways of the world. Unaware of the scheming and subterfuge that surrounded her, she simply did as she was told.

Soon after her wedding Jane became unwell. She wrote to a friend—Lady Letitia claimed to have seen the letter—that she believed her mother-in-law was trying to poison her. Apparently Jane had no knowledge of the *Device for the Succession,* or she would have known that she was far too valuable to be murdered.

On the fourth of July, I lay ill with a fever, perhaps brought on by the news delivered by Sir William. I had told no one save Kat of the *Device,* but it preyed on my mind. In this frail condition I received a message from

John Dudley: "His Majesty, the king, is near death. It is feared that he will not live out the week."

Numb and trembling, I called for Kat. "Edward is dying," I said tearfully. "What shall I do?"

"Wait," she advised. "You are too ill to travel, Elizabeth. Even if you were strong enough to leave at once, there is little prospect that you would arrive in time to see your dear brother alive. And," she added ominously, "this may well be a trap."

Of course! The fever had interfered with my thinking. Dudley might indeed be planning to lure my sister and me to London to make sure we were unable to interfere with his plans.

I accepted Kat's advice. I dispatched a message to my sister at her manor house in Hunsdon to inform her of my decision, but the messenger returned with word that Mary—usually wary of traps—had already left for Greenwich.

My brother, the king, died on Thursday, the sixth of July *anno Domini* 1553. As with the death of my father, news of his passing was suppressed for three days—not an easy task, given that the corpse had begun to rot in the summer heat. On Sunday, the ninth of July, a messenger in black crepe brought me official news of the death. I expected the news, but I had learned years earlier that even when death is anticipated, its reality and its finality still come as a shock.

In the days following Edward's death, events unfolded of which I had no knowledge at the time. Only later, when Sir William Cecil visited me at Hatfield, was I able to piece together what had happened. By then I was recovered from my fever and felt quite well again. I called for a refreshing drink to be brought to the knot garden while Sir William described to me the events of the past fortnight.

On the ninth of July, Lady Jane was taken to Syon House, one of the royal palaces, where her father-in-law knelt and solemnly informed her of the death of the king and of her succession. At this the entire company—including her hated mother-in-law—bowed down before her.

"Jane appeared stunned by this news," Cecil reported, "and she collapsed in a swoon. When she regained her senses, she burst into weeping and lamenting the death of the king. Then she told those around her in ringing tones—she has a remarkably strong voice for such a small person—that she did not want the crown. 'It pleases me not,' she said with great conviction. 'The lady Mary is the rightful heir.'"

"Poor Jane," I murmured. "She really did not want this."

But Dudley, with Jane's parents echoing his words, told her that she had nothing to say about it. "The king has willed it," said Dudley, "as God has willed it. You have no choice but to obey."

At last, Jane unhappily accepted. Hushed crowds gathered along the Thames to stare as the royal barge carried Jane and her retinue downriver to the Tower.

Cecil supplied me with all of the details, even down to her chopines, high wooden clogs strapped to her shoes to make her appear taller. Jane climbed clumsily up the stairs from the barge and tottered to the Tower and the royal apartments. She was told that she must stay there until her coronation.

"And when is that to be?" Jane asked.

"You will be informed when the time comes" was the reply.

When heralds were dispatched to proclaim the word throughout London that Jane Dudley was queen and Mary Tudor a bastard unfit to rule, there was no rejoicing. The announcement was greeted by the people with silence.

I listened attentively to all of this, outwardly calm and controlled. Inwardly, though, my head throbbed and my nerves were unstrung. "But where was Mary?" I asked Cecil hoarsely. "What of my sister?"

"While all of this was happening, Mary was en route to Greenwich. Along the way she encountered a messenger who warned her of danger. Robin Dudley was preparing to leave London with three hundred guardsmen to capture Mary and take her prisoner."

"My old friend Robin Dudley!" I felt my temper flare. "His deceitful father's deceitful son after all!"

"So it seems," Cecil said dryly. "But Lady Mary heeded the warning and immediately changed her plans. With only two ladies-in-waiting and a half dozen gentlemen, she fled through the night on horseback in the opposite direction.

"The next day—it was now the tenth of July— John Dudley informed Queen Jane that she must make her husband, Guildford, the king. Only twenty-four hours had passed, but by then she would have understood that John Dudley never intended for her to rule.

"Jane called together some of the privy councillors and told us, 'If the crown truly belongs to me, then I shall make my husband a duke. But I will not consent to make him king.'"

"She has more courage than I suspected."

"Jane has great courage," Cecil agreed. "This insolence was too much for her mother-in-law. Her fury barely contained, the duchess turned to Guildford and hissed, 'If she is stubborn, then you shall be just as stubborn. You must refuse to share a bed with this shrew you call wife!' Then the duchess stormed out of the room, with Guildford obediently following at her heels.

"That night we of the privy council received a letter from Mary, declaring her right to the throne. Robin Dudley had not been able to capture her after all! Lady Mary had arrived at Kenninghall, near Cambridge; she was free, and she was determined to be queen."

"Go on, go on!" I said, impatiently pacing the formal pattern of the knot garden.

"When John Dudley learned that powerful noblemen and common people alike were flocking to Mary's support, he prepared to fight. He assembled three thousand men at the Tower, armed with crossbows and pikes as well as cannons and gunpowder. He led his troops north toward Cambridge, boasting, 'I will put a quick end to Lady Mary's defiance.' But John Dudley forgot one thing: Mary is much loved, and nearly everyone hates him. Now, when he needed it most, the duke had no one he could trust."

"Good, good, good!" I cried.

"Hearing that John Dudley was on his way, Lady Mary left Cambridge and rode hard for East Anglia. Her castle at Framlingham is fortified with walls eight feet thick and forty feet high and watchtowers looking out to sea. As the news spread, people began to rally to her cause. Day after day they arrived, bringing whatever horses and arms they could muster, or sending carts of food and supplies. My messengers, quite breathless with the magnitude of it, reported to me that Lady Mary had somehow raised an army of twenty thousand! One after another the towns in the area proclaimed Mary as their queen."

"But what of John Dudley?" I asked.

"Things went badly for the duke. He had ordered seven warships to guard the coast to prevent Mary's escape, but the sailors mutinied. The next day two thousand seamen arrived at Mary's camp hauling a hundred enormous cannons from the ships.

"Imagine how uneasy the privy councillors felt! Most had sworn loyalty to Dudley. When it appeared that

Lady Mary might win after all, and knowing it would not go well for them if she did, they swung against Dudley. On the nineteenth every one of the councillors appeared in the public square and declared Mary our queen. Shortly thereafter, John Dudley gave up.

"There is nothing in memory equal to the celebration that began as soon as your sister was proclaimed," Cecil was saying. "The bells were ringing when I left, and may still be ringing, for all I know. The din was terrific! Men tossed their caps into the air and cheered, and women wept for joy. The jubilant throngs were preparing to feast and dance and sing all night."

So my sister was now queen. And because she had triumphed *I was next*! This was the moment, standing in the knot garden, when I realized that someday I, too, would become queen of England. How I savored that moment! As I listened to Cecil's description, I saw myself in Mary's place, the bells ringing, the crowds cheering. *Someday...*

"The scene must have been quite different at the Tower of London," I observed, bringing myself back to the moment.

Sir William stroked his close-trimmed beard. "Ah, poor little Queen Jane," he sighed. "There she sat, pale as death, waiting with her father for the outcome. When Lord Grey learned that all of the councillors had turned against Dudley, he rushed out and made a great show of proclaiming Mary the queen. Then he returned to the royal apartments and tore down the cloth of estate that had been hung above his daughter's chair and ordered her to remove her royal robes. She was queen for just nine days."

"What will happen to her now?" I asked, imagining myself in Jane's stead, both relieved and frightened, in equal parts.

"She will be locked up in the Tower, along with her husband," said Sir William. "But I cannot imagine that Queen Mary will be anything other than forgiving. Lady Jane has no fault in this."

I said nothing, silently praying that he was right.

Sir William drained his cup and begged my leave. He was on his way to Framlingham Castle to pledge his loyalty to Queen Mary. "I suspect that many from the privy council will be there, humbly begging her pardon, on their knees in the hope of saving their necks."

I asked him to tarry long enough for me to send a letter with him for Mary, offering my sister my congratulations at the same time that I expressed my sorrow at the death of our brother. But even as I wrote, somewhere in my mind the thought lingered, *Someday it will be my turn.*

WHEN ALL THE rebels had been rounded up and hauled off to cells in the Tower, Mary set out from Framlingham with an escort of several thousand men. With great excitement I rode out to meet the new queen, accompanied by my own retinue of a thousand knights, gentlemen, and ladies-in-waiting. As Mary approached I climbed down from my horse and knelt in the dusty road. When she saw me, Mary immediately dismounted and raised me up.

I had not seen my sister for five years, and I believe we were each surprised by the appearance of the other. Mary was thirty-seven, an aging woman, while I was not yet twenty. For a moment we stared at each other, and then Mary kissed me. After she had embraced me, the queen went to the gentlewomen in my retinue and embraced each one.

As I watched Mary I did wonder if she saw me as a rival. I wished I could reassure her that she had nothing to fear from me. In the natural course of events, my turn would inevitably come. I would not challenge her. I had only to wait.

Together we rode side by side toward London, banners fluttering and horns blaring fanfares. Outside the city the great procession halted so that Mary could change out of her dusty clothing.

Queen Mary entered the capital dressed in a gown of purple velvet over a petticoat of purple satin stitched with goldwork and pearls. More gems ornamented her velvet sleeves and headdress, and the baldric she wore draped across her chest. Even her horse was gorgeously arrayed, trapped in embroidered cloth of gold. The train of Mary's gown was so long and so heavy that it had to be carried on the shoulder of one of the gentlemen of her household.

I had never seen such a public outpouring of affection, and I was excited and proud to be in a place of honor on that day of my sister's triumph. A tide of loving emotion swept over us as we slowly followed her through the city, stopping often to listen to choirs singing songs of praise. As we neared the Tower, cannons thundered so loudly that the ground shook and windowpanes shattered. At last Queen Mary entered the royal apartments so recently vacated by Queen Jane, now kept prisoner in another part of the Tower.

On the first of October in 1553, wearing a crimson robe trimmed with ermine over my gown of white and silver, I carried my sister's train at her coronation. The pomp and ceremony exceeded even that of Edward's coronation, for the new queen had a flair for pageantry. After a ceremony lasting seven hours, I was the first to take the oath of allegiance to Queen Mary. At the banquet that followed at Westminster Hall, I was seated next to my sister. Thousands of dishes had been prepared for the feast, but the queen ate only the wild boar. These exhilarating days were a time of joy and celebration for everyone—everyone save those shut up in the Tower.

I, too, rejoiced: *I shall be the next queen of England! I shall be the next to wear the crown!*

CHAPTER 8

Queen Mary

After her coronation Mary moved from her country manor into Whitehall Palace. Soon thereafter she invited me to join her at court. After all those months in the country, I was happy to take up residence in London. I settled into Somerset House, the city mansion I had acquired after the execution of its former owner, Edward Seymour, duke of Somerset. I had traded another property for this great mansion, which was much to my taste—a combination of classic simplicity and elegance. It was also close to Whitehall.

One afternoon the queen's messenger delivered a note. I broke the royal seal. *Dearest Sister,* the note began. *We beg you to sup with us this day. We have much to discuss with you.* It was signed *Maria Regina*—Mary the Queen.

I understood that she was using the royal *we*. And I wondered what it was *we* wanted to discuss. While the messenger waited, I penned a quick reply, assuring Her Majesty of my great pleasure, and so on and so forth.

I was in a fine mood as I prepared to take supper with the queen. Kat Ashley watched as my maids dressed me in a black velvet gown with French sleeves over a white damask petticoat. Kat was no longer with me as a governess—I was now twenty—but I relied on her as I always had for her companionship.

"No jewels, madam?" asked Kat, who was always urging me to wear one of the finely wrought pieces left me by my father. "The diamond-and-ruby necklace would be splendid with that gown."

"No jewels," I said firmly, still feeling that a plain form of dress suited me best. Instead, around my waist I clasped a simple gold chain from which hung a girdle book, a miniature prayer book bound in gold. It had been a gift from my brother, and I treasured it. Then I called for Lady Marian and Lady Cynthia to accompany me and two gentlemen to ride with us to Whitehall Palace.

Ushered into the queen's privy chamber, I dropped three times to one knee (Mary didn't require this be done five times, as Edward had) as I approached her chair. After we had exchanged the usual greetings, Queen Mary invited me to be seated on a low stool, my ladies on silken cushions with her ladies. Then she called for wine to be brought.

I had scarcely taken the first sip from the golden goblet when Mary looked at me steadily and said in her deep, resonant voice, "And are you hearing Mass regularly, Elizabeth?"

"I attend those services that it so pleases God for me to attend," I replied with care, "and I am down on my knees in our Lord's presence at every opportunity."

She knew the answer to her question before she asked it, and I knew that my evasive words didn't please her.

"We are sure you know, my lady Elizabeth, that we intend to restore the old religion as quickly as possible."

King Henry had banned the Catholic Church, and now Queen Mary made it plain that she intended to bring back the Roman Catholic faith to England. I didn't see how Mary had the right to undo everything our father and brother had done.

"But, Your Majesty," I replied, perhaps too hastily, "your first official announcement granted your subjects the freedom to worship as they choose."

The queen peered at me, head cocked to one side. "To show our good intentions, did we not order two funerals to be held for our dear brother, a Protestant service at Westminster Abbey, and a requiem Mass at the White Tower?"

"Yes, madam," I said. I did not add that I had naively assumed she meant to permit the two faiths to exist side by side for a much longer time.

Mary gazed at me with glittering eyes. "Now, who better to assist in making the change—the *necessary* change—than the queen's own sister?"

"Yes, madam," I repeated meekly. I saw that it was useless—even dangerous—to argue.

"Good," said the queen. "Half a dozen Masses are said daily in our chapel royal. Every one of our privy councillors attends. We expect that you will attend as well, Elizabeth."

"Yes, madam."

"And stop wearing that foolish prayer book you have hanging at your waist," she said irritably.

"As Your Majesty wishes," I said. What else is there to say to the queen? One may disagree, but one obeys. Or gives the impression of obedience. *Oh, to be queen and have such power!* I thought.

Then Mary presented me with a gift, a rosary with beads of red and white coral, and proceeded with our supper—stew made of wild boar, of which I am not overfond but that was apparently my sister's favorite dish.

Throughout the meal we were entertained by the antics of Jane the Fool. She was dressed as a lady of the court in silks and satins, but for her shoes and stockings, which were those of a clown. With her shaved head and odd costume, Jane looked absurd.

To my great relief the evening ended early. I could hardly wait to get away from my sister.

"We shall be attending Mass," I told my ladies as we

rode back to Somerset House. "Every morning, every evening, and sometimes in between."

"Yes, madam," they murmured.

"If you do not know how to say a rosary," I said, "then you had better learn."

KAT WAS ANXIOUSLY pacing my bedchamber. I removed my girdle book, kissed it in memory of Edward, and handed it to her. "I am forbidden to wear this," I told her.

As my maids undressed me, I described the conversation with the queen.

"It is no small thing that she requires of you," Kat said, "but you can in your heart make it seem but a small thing. For your own safety and good."

And so, with a great show of piety, I presented myself twice each day at Mass at one of the chapels royal, where I would be publicly observed and my presence quickly reported to Mary, if she happened not to be there. I carried the rosary she had given me and murmured my prayers over the beads as I counted them one by one. I fixed my eyes upon the jeweled crosses that had been placed once more upon the altars, along with the gold candlesticks and chalices set with precious gems, now brought out of those secret places where they had been hidden during Edward's reign.

I went to Mass only because I was forced to. When I found an excuse—a headache, a stomach pain, a touch of choler—I did not attend. My ladies-in-waiting were instructed to make known to Mary's ladies-in-waiting that I suffered from an indisposition of some sort.

I tried to give the appearance of conforming to the queen's doctrines, but I still believed as I had always believed. Mary was not deceived. It was the loyal Sir William Cecil who warned me: "The queen knows well enough that your behavior is a pretense, and the sham infuriates her. She makes no secret of her dislike of you and speaks of it openly, as do the visitors to her court. You are referred to as 'the heretic sister.'"

"And what of you, Sir William?" I retorted. "Are you not a heretic as well?"

"I am not a Catholic, that is true. And I am no longer a member of the privy council, although I have placed myself at the queen's service. But I do not challenge her rule. You do, madam." As we parted Cecil bowed low. "Spies are all around you," he murmured. "Take care."

The queen and I continued to treat each other with icy civility. We were both good actors, but I was better—I had to be.

When the queen called her first Parliament, she demanded that her mother's marriage to our father be declared lawful. This officially removed the stain of bastardy from Mary. But she had no intention of doing the same favor for my mother and me. If she had her way, I would remain a bastard all my life.

I HAD JUST returned from Mass early one morning when one of my young pages announced a visitor. "Edward Courtenay, earl of Devon," piped the boy. Lady Cynthia and Lady Letitia glanced up, surprised at a caller's coming at such an hour.

The words were scarcely out of the page's mouth than the earl pranced into my chambers, without waiting for permission or invitation. He was foppishly dressed in brown velvet trunk hose slashed to reveal yellow satin. A great many pearls were stitched to his velvet doublet, and a yellow feather drooped from his cap. "Good morrow, Lady Elizabeth," he said, as though we had known each other all our lives and were on familiar terms. He did not doff his cap, nor did he bow as deeply as he should have.

Startled, I dropped the book I was reading. He picked it up and handed it to me, grinning broadly.

I snatched the book out of his hand. "To what do I owe the honor of your presence, *Mister* Courtenay?" I asked coldly.

He opened his arms expansively. "Queen Mary has set me free! She sent me these clothes, and many more like them, and she gave me a title, earl of Devon. And plenty of jewels, too. Look"—he waved a ring beneath my nose—"she gave me this as well." The ring that glittered on his finger had once belonged to my father. I scarcely knew whether to laugh in his face or have him removed from my sight.

I had never met Edward Courtenay before, although I had heard of him. Many years earlier my father had ordered the execution of Courtenay's father and had young Edward shut up in the Tower of London, where he'd remained a prisoner for fifteen years. He was now twenty-seven.

In the years he'd spent behind prison walls, Courtenay had become an accomplished scholar and musician. During his visit he quoted intelligently and at length from works of Cicero. Then, without so much as a by-your-leave, he picked up my lute and entertained us with a few songs. Apparently no one had taught him manners. I could not understand the purpose of his visit and found his presence exceedingly annoying. It was all I could do to get rid of him.

The door was hardly shut behind him than Lady Letitia jumped up and began to mimic his preening walk and extravagant gestures. "Poor fellow! Poor fellow!" cried Lady Marian, and we all laughed until we wept at the unfortunate Courtenay.

"Watch out, madam," sniffed Lady Cynthia, dabbing tears from her eyes. "Next he will be coming to court you!"

"I should hope not!" I exclaimed. But I did wonder if the queen had sent him to visit with a plan in mind.

ONE DAY IN October I received a letter from my cousin Catherine Knollys. Catherine was the daughter of my mother's sister, Mary Carey. Catherine had married Sir Francis Knollys, a pompous man with a reputation as a fanatical Protestant. Sir Francis was much older than Catherine, and I thought the match a very dull one. Catherine doted on her young daughter, a child I had not seen since her christening.

"My dear cousin," wrote Catherine from her estate in Essex, "too long a time has passed since last we enjoyed one another's company. I beg your leave to allow me a visit."

I replied at once, bidding her to come without delay and to bring her darling little Lettice.

Catherine arrived in mid-October with only a governess for the little girl and three servants, almost as though the visit were secret.

My cousin had become rounder in face and figure since the birth of her daughter, but she also looked tired and drawn. Lettice was an exquisite child, barely five years old, with reddish curls and great blue eyes. My servants offered comfits to the daughter and hippocras to the mother, who drank it off greedily. Then Catherine set down the goblet with a nervous clank.

"May we speak freely?" she asked in a low voice.

I didn't answer directly. "If you are not too weary from your journey," I said, rising, "you and Lettice might enjoy a walk in the garden."

I knew that Mary had placed a number of spies in my household, adding to my discomfort, but I hadn't yet discovered which servants were loyal to me and which would betray me and my friends. In the garden at least, Catherine and I would be alone—observed, no doubt, but not overheard.

Soon we were strolling arm in arm, and Lettice gamboled like a spring lamb along the paths. The air was soft and unusually warm. "Now, dear cousin," I said, "tell me."

Catherine stared straight ahead. "We are leaving."

"Leaving?" For a moment I thought she meant that she and Lettice were cutting short their visit. "But you have only just arrived. Leaving for where?"

"France. My husband says we have no choice. The queen has made it impossible for us to stay here."

I understood; Sir Francis was outspoken in his religious views. I said nothing but patted her arm as comfortingly as I knew how.

"We expect the persecution to begin sooner rather than later," Catherine continued. "We are fleeing for our lives, Elizabeth, and so should you!" she added passionately.

"Have no fear for me," I assured her, although I felt far from assured myself. "I attend Mass regularly. The queen knows this."

"That is not enough to protect you," Catherine declared. "Many other Protestants are leaving for the Continent, and we are prepared to stay abroad for as long as Mary is queen. But many more will remain here, and they are as unhappy as we that our freedom to worship is being taken away."

I nodded. "Perhaps the queen will relent when she sees how many oppose her." I didn't believe that, but I did not want to reveal my own deep fears.

Catherine stopped and gripped both of my hands in hers. "Why are you being so blind, Elizabeth? The Protestants who stay here will surely plot a rebellion against Queen Mary—Francis has told me that. They will just as surely rally around you, and you will be blamed!"

"I will have nothing to do with such a plot," I said.

"You will have nothing to say about it, and Queen Mary will not take your word. Your house is infested with spies!" Catherine was weeping now. "Oh, dear Elizabeth, I fear that I shall never see you again!"

The sound of her mother's sobs attracted the notice of little Lettice, who scampered back to clutch at Catherine's petticoats. I pressed my fingers to my cousin's lips, begging her to say no more. We finished our walk and returned to the palace, holding tightly to each other's hands to still the trembling.

Catherine and Lettice stayed with me for three days. Naturally I wanted to question Catherine at length: Did she know of any such plots? Did she know the names of the plotters? Had my name been mentioned, or was this simply a guess? But I decided that it was safer if I did *not* know. Then, if questioned, I could truthfully plead complete innocence.

At the end of the three days, my cousin prepared to leave, all of us weeping many tears, not knowing when—or if!—we would see one another again. Catherine tried once more to persuade me to flee to the safety of the Continent.

"I cannot leave England," I told her. "I *am* England, and someday I shall be her queen."

"But you must *live* if you are to become queen!" she cried.

"I shall live and I shall rule," I said. But at that moment I needed every bit of courage to believe my own words.

CHAPTER 9

The Queen in Love

M y heart still ached from the departure of my cousin Catherine when Queen Mary startled us all with the announcement that she had decided the time had come for her to marry. She informed the privy council of her intent, and now the talk was of little else.

"Marry!" I exclaimed to Sir William Cecil when he brought me this latest piece of news. "Marry *whom*?"

It was believed that no woman had the wit or the strength to rule on her own—even Sir William was in agreement with that notion. The choice of a husband for the queen, then, was of the greatest importance, not merely for her own happiness but for the good of the country. Almost from the moment the crown had settled upon Mary's head, a number of suitors had appeared. But Mary had shown no interest in any of them and no inclination to proceed quickly, and so the new announcement came as a surprise.

Over supper Sir William and I considered the possibilities.

"Reginald Pole," suggested Sir William.

"Pole is a cardinal!" I protested. "A prince of the Catholic Church! He has been in Rome since my father banished him twenty years ago. And was he not within a vote or two of being elected pope?"

Sir William fingered his tidy mustache. "All that you say is true. But Pole was never ordained a priest. He is only a deacon, and he might, if he wishes—if the queen wishes—be released from his deacon's vows."

"I have heard that Mary once loved him," I said, considering the idea. "But that was years ago."

"There is another candidate," Cecil continued. "And he has the backing of many on the privy council."

"And who may that be?"

"Edward Courtenay."

I burst out laughing. Since his visit to me, I'd had no private meetings with the earl, but he had certainly been visible at court.

"He struts about like a peacock, well pleased with himself," I reminded Cecil, "and he has not the least idea of proper behavior. I suppose it is difficult to learn courtly manners when one has been shut away from society throughout one's youth, but I suspect that Edward Courtenay might have been just as insufferable if he had been brought up at the king's elbow."

Cecil agreed, but he pointed out that even with all his faults, there were councillors who thought Courtenay the best match for the queen. "He is English, and his bloodlines are good—that is enough to convince the council, who would do anything to avoid having a foreigner as king. But," continued Cecil, "the queen will learn soon enough that Courtenay has been seen in the company of loose women and has a talent for debauchery. The earl of Devon will no longer be a contender for the queen's hand."

"Or for mine, thank goodness," I put in. "Who is your next guess, then?"

"Philip of Spain."

"Surely not!" I exclaimed. "I care not a whit whom my sister marries, but I cannot imagine that she would take a Spaniard as her consort. He will be despised by every person with English blood in his veins!"

But Sir William's last guess proved correct: Queen Mary's choice fell upon the Spanish prince, the son of her mother's cousin, Emperor Charles V.

Mary had once been betrothed by our father to Charles, when she was but six years old and Charles was twenty-two. The betrothal had been broken, and Charles married someone else, by whom he had a son, Philip. Prince Philip was now twenty-seven, ten years younger than Mary.

Said Cecil, "It is only a matter of time until Mary will be shoved into the background and Philip will rule. Her advisers are warning her of this, but she pays no attention."

"And what is her reply?"

"That this marriage is God's will. Her mother was Spanish, her ties with the emperor are strong, and she feels called to marry Philip."

My stubborn sister! No one could tell her anything. As I expected, the announcement of Mary's betrothal upset nearly everyone.

"I detest the Spaniards," Kat grumbled. "Imagine Philip coming here and taking over our country! Having sovereignty over us! The queen is making a dreadful mistake."

A few weeks after Mary announced her intention, a large portrait of Philip arrived at Whitehall. Queen Mary invited me and a number of her ladies to view the likeness. The painting was set upon an easel in the queen's presence chamber, covered with a cloth of purple silk. Lady Marian and Lady Cynthia accompanied me, and as we waited for the queen to appear, we kept our eyes on the purple cloth. There was a stir, and we dropped to our knees as the door opened.

As usual the queen was gowned in rich velvet trimmed in brocade and decked with more jewels than I could count. She sparkled from head to toe, and her eyes seemed to sparkle as well. She swept aside the purple silk and stepped back, and we all gaped at the portrait. "Our future husband," she said, for once sounding shy.

The young prince, dressed in a blue coat trimmed with white wolf skin, was a man well made in face and figure. I could understand her attraction to him, based on that likeness.

Has anyone sent Philip a portrait of Mary? I wondered. *What will he think when he sees this aging queen? Might he change his mind?* I remembered my father's response to Anne of Cleves.

No matter what our private thoughts, we ladies all applauded enthusiastically and murmured approvingly. "The prince is now three years older since he posed for the artist Titian," she explained. "We are told he has developed an even more manly body. And a fuller beard," she added, blushing.

"I give not a fig what he looks like," Lady Cynthia muttered gloomily as we rode back to Somerset House. "He is still a Spaniard."

"Perhaps she has no choice," said Lady Marian with a sigh. "She must marry someone, and it might as well be he."

She can remain unwed, I thought. *That is what I intend to do.* But these were not thoughts I wished to speak aloud.

MY HOPE THAT my sister's coming marriage might distract her attention from me proved groundless.

First she sent a note that I was to have no more

visitors without her approval. Once again Kat caught the full force of my fury.

"How dare she!" I shouted. "She treats me like a common criminal!"

Kat had no answer but the obvious one: "She dares because she is queen."

Then Mary sent me books of instruction in the Catholic faith. I flung them against the wall but retrieved them quickly, aware—belatedly—that spies were rewarded for passing on just such bits of information. I reminded myself that I must keep my temper and hold my tongue, no matter how sorely I was tested.

On a day when a sharp wind warned of coming winter, the queen summoned me once more to her presence chamber. I dreaded this interview; perhaps she had heard of my outburst and intended to chastise me. I dropped to one knee, advanced a step, dropped again, advanced, dropped a third time.

"Dear sister," said Queen Mary in a chilly voice.

"Your Majesty," I replied.

"You have been attending Mass daily, have you not?"

"I have, Your Majesty. *Twice* daily. Surely you have heard reports of this?" I knew that she had. It seemed to me that half of my servants and even a number of my ladies and gentlemen were spies who eagerly poured what they'd seen or heard, or thought they had, into Mary's ear.

"We know well that your *person* has been present at the Mass. But what of your mind? Your heart, Elizabeth?

Your *soul?*" She smiled sourly. "That is where we have our doubts."

"But, Your Majesty, I am most sincere in my faith," I protested.

"Do you firmly believe what Catholics believe— have always believed?" she demanded, leaning forward intently.

To be honest was to risk what freedom I did have, and possibly even my life. And so I choked back what I wanted to say: *One cannot be forced to believe what one does not believe!* I swore that I did believe, that I attended Mass of my own free will and with genuine faith. I knelt with my hands clasped upon my heart as I spoke, to add feeling to my statement. To my lies.

"We hear no truth in your words," Mary said coldly. She leaned back abruptly. "You are far too much like your mother. You become more like her every day—a woman who caused much trouble in the kingdom."

At the insult to my mother, my intense dislike of Mary exploded into hatred. I felt my cheeks flame, but I was careful to betray none of my anger in my voice or manner. "I beg you to remember, Your Majesty, that you and I have the same father. The same Tudor blood runs thick in our veins."

Mary laughed, a harsh, unpleasant sound. "There is some question about that," she said, tapping her fingers on the arms of her chair.

I held myself rigid and simply stared at her, scarcely daring to breathe.

"It is evident that you bear far more resemblance to the lowborn Mark Smeaton than ever you have to the man you call father," she said.

I was so angry I feared I might faint, and I reached out a hand to steady myself. But I was also, suddenly, greatly frightened. Mark Smeaton was one of the five men with whom my mother had been wrongfully accused of committing adultery against my father. The other four were gentlemen—one, my mother's own brother!—and all were ordered beheaded by my father. My mother was forced to watch them die before she, too, went to the block.

Mary knew that the charges against Anne Boleyn were lies, fabrications my father used to rid himself of the wife he no longer wanted. But now it was as though not I but my mother knelt before Mary, facing her judgment. Would her actions be as cruel as her words? Trembling, I waited.

For a long moment the queen stared at me. Then abruptly she dismissed me with a wave of her hand. I backed away, kneeling three times as I did, my legs so weak I thought I might not be able to rise again. It was all I could do to walk steadily past Jane the Fool with her shaved head, past the queen's ladies-in-waiting, who sat placidly with their embroidery on their laps. Past the guards standing stiffly at each door, past the gentlemen who idled about in the long gallery, past the guards posted at Whitehall's entrance.

Expecting the queen's guards to seize me, I waited, breathing in ragged gasps while my horse was brought to the courtyard. Although I wanted desperately to give my horse full rein, I maintained a measured gait all the way back to my own palace. Each step carried me away from the hateful queen but not, I feared, away from danger.

WHEN I ARRIVED at Somerset House, I first had to acknowledge the salutes of the guards, the gentlemen who attended me, the servants, my own ladies-in-waiting. My legs were still weak, but I held myself erect and walked to my bedchamber, pretending nothing was wrong. As soon as the door shut behind me, I flung myself upon my bed and wept until I was wrung dry of tears.

Then anger overcame fear. I leaped up and called for Kat.

After I had described the scene with the queen, Kat said, "You must go away from here. The sooner the better. You are in danger of your very life, Elizabeth. This is not simply some inconvenience of where and how you worship."

I considered Kat's advice. "You are right," I agreed, and the next day I sent a letter to my sister. "I beg Your Majesty's leave to remove my household to Ashridge in Hertfordshire," I wrote.

For days I waited for a reply. When it came, the answer was no.

I wrote again, imploring her to grant me an audience. Anxious days passed. Finally the queen agreed to see me.

As I knelt before her in an attitude of supplication, Mary gazed at me for a long time. In my heart I was furious, but I could not reveal any of that anger.

"You wish to leave court?" she asked finally.

"If Your Grace will grant me leave," I whispered, "I wish to move to Ashridge."

"You may go," she said at last.

I thanked her—at least I meant *that*! When I rose and prepared to depart, kneeling, backing, kneeling, the queen stopped me. "Elizabeth!"

I waited nervously for what might come.

"Before you leave London," she said, "we should like to meet with you once more."

"As Your Majesty desires," I replied, and knelt a third time.

WHAT MORE *does she want?* I worried as my servants completed preparations for the move. I sent word to the queen that I would wait upon her when she wished. The next day she sent for me. I tried to prepare myself for what I hoped would be a last visit.

This time Mary seemed more at ease, almost friendly. I didn't trust her friendliness. Jane the Fool and Lucretia the Tumbler were both present, distracting the queen with their antics. Jane, I observed, looked different; a luxurious hood made of sable covered her usually naked head.

"We have a gift for you," said Queen Mary. Immediately Jane the Fool stepped forward, capering in her foolish clown shoes, and flung off the hood. Mary took the hood from her and draped it about my head and shoulders. "To ward off the frosts of winter at Ashridge," said the queen.

An instant later Lucretia the Tumbler performed a somersault and some sleight of hand in front of me, and I found myself holding two strings of costly pearls. I looked up in wonder. Mary smiled, but her eyes remained cold. "These gifts are so that you do not forget us," she said.

"You will never be far from my thoughts, dear sister," I said. True enough—I would always be fearful of her, and I would never cease to hate her.

Queen Mary rose and embraced me. I forced myself to return the embrace. She gave me her blessing, and I was dismissed. I was free to go.

But my relief was short-lived. Outside the queen's privy chamber door, two of her councillors, Sir William Paget and the earl of Arundel, lay in wait.

"Lady Elizabeth," said Paget, his words and tone pointedly reminding me that in the eyes of many I was not a princess but the bastard daughter of a disgraced woman.

One on either side of me, they escorted me down

the long gallery and pulled me into an empty chamber. The heavy door slammed shut. Both looked grim. What did these two want of me?

"You leave shortly for Ashridge?" Paget asked.

"On the morrow."

"Who accompanies you?"

Kat, I told them. Mr. Parry, my cofferer, and his sister Blanche, who chaperoned the maids. I named off others of my suite, growing increasingly fearful.

"And who awaits you there?" asked Arundel.

I looked at him, frankly puzzled. "And who *should* be awaiting me there?" I asked, turning the question back on him.

The councillors exchanged glances. "We shall be more honest with you than you have perhaps been with us," Paget said. "This is a warning, my lady Elizabeth: You will be watched closely for any sign that you might be planning a rising, a rebellion designed to overthrow the queen."

"I assure you that I have no such intent, my lords," I said, quite honestly, for I did not. "My loyalty is entirely with my sister, the queen, whom I love and honor."

"Mind, then, that you do not become involved in someone else's intentions. You may be innocent, but there are others who are not. Responsibility for any treasonous act will fall upon your shoulders."

The two old windbags stepped back, bowed, and allowed me to leave the chamber. I fled with as much appearance of calm as I could muster, far more than I felt.

THICK FLAKES of an early snow began to fall as I left London late in November. Peasants and yeomen stepped off the muddy road to make way for the royal entourage and touched their caps respectfully. When I arrived at Ashridge, my first duty was to write to the queen, thanking her for her many kindnesses. But I also asked that she send the priestly vestments needed for the celebration of Mass. Mary had seen to it that several Catholic priests were included in my retinue, and I wanted to have them properly attired for their role as I continued to play *my* role as a make-believe Catholic.

Then I settled down to spend what I hoped would be a peaceful winter, with my usual quiet pursuits of study, embroidery, music, and conversation with my ladies.

CHAPTER 10

Rebellion
and Treachery

*S*oon after my arrival at Ashridge, a strange thing happened. I was in the chapel, kneeling behind the screen to make my confession, when a messenger disguised as a priest delivered me a letter. *To Elizabeth, the true and only princess fit to rule England,* the letter began. *Your day will come soon. Preparations have begun. Pray for our success. Your obedient servant, Thomas Wyatt.*

My heart raced. I had only slight knowledge of this Wyatt. But though I was in the chapel, I silently cursed him. What he had done was terribly dangerous—to himself, certainly, and no less to me.

"I can have no part in this," I whispered to the priest-messenger in the confessional and quickly fled from the chapel. I destroyed the letter immediately and spoke of it to no one—not even Kat. And, only half believing the good intentions of this Wyatt, son of a great poet in my father's court, I tried to put it from my mind and prayed that the plot would go no further. When I heard nothing more, I began to breathe more easily.

As winter deepened I fell ill with fevers and took to my bed. Kat, alarmed by my weakness and pallor, summoned my physician, who diagnosed an excess of choler.

When various unpleasant purgatives brought no improvement, the physician consulted my astrologer, Dr. John Dee, who determined that bleeding in the hour after midnight would cure me. A surgeon was summoned to open the vein in my left arm. After the basin of blood had been carried away and my wound bound up, Kat fed me teas made with herbs and kept close watch over me. At last the fever left me, but I still did not have the strength to stand unaided.

As I began to recover, Kat sat by my bedside and described all that had happened during the days that I drifted in and out of my feverish dreams.

"Diplomats arrived from Spain to conclude the marriage negotiations between Prince Philip and the queen," she told me. "Their welcome was cold. Mr. Parry heard that they were greeted with snowballs hurled, along with unkind words, by Englishmen who want no part of a Spanish king."

I smiled at that—the haughty Spanish pelted with snowballs! "When do they intend to marry?" I asked.

"In summer, I believe. But there is another story, far more serious," Kat continued. "On the twenty-fifth of January, Sir Thomas Wyatt of Kent raised up an army of several thousand men and marched toward London, intent upon seizing the queen."

"What happened?" I asked, instantly alert. *The letter!* I thought.

"When word spread of Wyatt's rebellion, many urged the queen to take shelter within the walls of the Tower. Some even tried to persuade her to flee the country. But she refused to do any of this. Instead, she stood steadfast. The queen made a brave speech that Mr. Parry says brought tears to all who heard, and they pledged to support her."

"But surely the rising failed?"

"It did. Wyatt was captured on the seventh of February and is being held in the Tower." Kat hesitated, but I pressed her to continue, ordering her to tell me everything.

"Wyatt claims he did it for you, that you knew all along about the plans, and that you had given your consent to his cause—even your support."

"Lies!" I exclaimed, although they were not exactly. "All lies!" I struggled to sit up, but the effort exhausted me, and I fell back upon my pillows. "Did he act alone?" I asked. "Were there others?"

"Edward Courtenay has also been arrested."

"Courtenay, too? That idiot! What was his role in this pitiable mummery?"

"The plot was to marry you to Courtenay and to place you both on the throne in Mary's stead."

My mind reeled. It was almost too much to take in. "Is there more?" I asked, hoping there was not.

"I fear so, madam."

"Then tell me!"

"It is Lady Jane Dudley and her husband, Guildford," Kat said sadly. "The queen has signed the order for their execution."

"But surely they had no part in this conspiracy!"

"No, madam, they did not," Kat said. "But Jane's father did. They found him hiding in a hollow tree. It is all done for them, I fear."

I turned my head away. My sister would actually have this young woman beheaded? Surely not! It was not Jane's doing! But even in my enfeebled state, I was certain of one thing: Mary would lay the blame at my feet, and I would pay dearly for all that had happened. If she would send Lady Jane to the scaffold, Mary would not hesitate to send me. Clearly the queen was afraid, and fear had made her ruthless. I was tired, so very tired, but I realized that I would soon have to gather every ounce of strength I possessed to defend myself— or lose my life.

THE TIME CAME before I was ready. The fever had returned and was worse than ever, and I had not left my bedchamber in weeks. One morning as I lay in bed in great discomfort, I heard a commotion below and was told that a messenger had arrived from London. He insisted upon delivering a letter to me in person. As he entered my chamber, I saw that he was garbed in the queen's livery. My heart pounded as I broke the wax seal impressed with the queen's device.

The lady Elizabeth is commanded to present herself without delay to Her Majesty, the queen. Nothing more—no explanation, no reason given. It was signed, with her initials, *M. R.*, for Maria Regina.

I fell back upon my pillows, and Kat took the letter from my hand. "Nonsense!" she scolded the messenger. "You can see for yourself that the lady Elizabeth is in no condition to travel."

But the messenger met Kat's stubborn resistance with his own stubbornness: I must prepare to leave at once. The queen had ordered it, and I must obey.

Kat refused to yield, and I was too ill to do more than protest ineffectually. Kat swept out of my chamber in search of my physicians and instructed them to write to Queen Mary at once. Within the hour the messenger was on his way to London with the physicians' letter. At least I would gain a little time, but I was sleepless with worry.

In less than a week, a second messenger appeared. The fever had subsided, and I was recovered enough to be propped on pillows. But I was still weak as a newborn. This second messenger was accompanied by stern-faced guards.

"Our orders are to take the lady Elizabeth by force if

necessary," said the captain of the guards, a burly man with an ill-trimmed beard.

"Away with you!" Kat ordered, shooing the guards as though they were a flock of geese. "The lady is ill and needs time to prepare."

"Mary does not believe that I am ill," I said tearfully to Kat when the guards had reluctantly withdrawn. "She thinks I feign illness to win her sympathy."

"Dear Elizabeth," Kat said, "you have no choice but to make the journey. The queen has sent a litter for you, and the guards will brook no refusal or delay. I shall accompany you to make sure that every care is taken."

And so, on the eighteenth of February, terrified of what lay ahead, I left Ashridge with my entourage. Usually the journey to London in a litter took three days, although the time was far less on a fast horse. But Kat, riding beside me in the litter, grimly refused to allow the horsemen to move at any but the slowest pace. With all the halts and rests required for even minimal comfort, the journey lasted five days. For me it was five days of misery.

As we approached London I summoned enough strength to have my maids dress me in a pure white gown. The queen's guard approached to escort us the rest of the way, and Kat drew back the curtains of the litter so that the curious crowds gathered along our route might see for themselves how ill I was. And in truth I had never felt worse in my life.

I assumed that I would be taken to Whitehall Palace to meet with my sister, but I was wrong. I was taken instead to St. James's Palace, where I was placed under guard. The captain of the guards read off the names of a half dozen of my ladies. "You are permitted to stay with the lady Elizabeth," he informed them brusquely. "The rest of you are ordered to leave at once."

I gasped. In confusion, the ladies who had been dismissed began to gather their belongings. Kat refused to move, and one of the guards shoved her rudely.

"I did not hear my name read out," she said loudly, "but surely that is an omission."

The guard glared at her. "You must be Mistress Ashley. It is the queen's specific order that you are dismissed."

Kat cried out, and although I felt like screaming, I merely embraced her as hard as I could and then watched her go. Both of us choked back tears.

Soon another half dozen ladies arrived, women I believed were picked by Mary to spy upon me. Lady Maud, a wizened dame of advanced years, was more talkative than the others. From her I heard the sad news that Lady Jane and Guildford Dudley had been beheaded.

"I was with her to the end, poor brave soul," Lady Maud said in her cracked voice. "And the queen gave her every chance to live." Maud shook a gnarled finger at me. "Her Majesty even offered Lady Jane a reprieve, if she would only profess the Catholic faith. But Lady

Jane would have none of it. She spent her last hours writing letters to her family and composing the speech she would utter from the scaffold itself."

I thought of the brilliant but serious girl who had shared my tutors. *Would I have had her courage? Will I need it in what lies ahead?*

"Then the queen granted a request from Guildford to bid his wife farewell," said Maud. "But Lady Jane refused to see him. Not being of royal blood, he was marched off to Tower Hill for his execution. I was with Lady Jane when the cart brought his headless body wrapped in a bloody sheet on its way to burial. She turned quite pale, I can tell you, but even then she did not cry out."

I thought of Guildford Dudley, a callow and simpering youth whom I'd never much liked. Lady Maud clearly relished this opportunity to tell her tale, and I did not interrupt her.

"It was my duty to follow Lady Jane up the steps of the scaffold, and I did as I must, although my heart was breaking for her. She knelt down in the sawdust and recited the Fifty-first Psalm, beginning to end. Handing me her gloves and her handkerchief, she took the blindfold and tied it over her own eyes, refusing my assistance. But then she could not see to find her way to the block, and groped for it like a blind person. 'Where is it? Where is it?' she cried. It fell to me to guide her to it, although I would have done anything in the world not to."

Lady Maud paused to snuffle into her handkerchief before she continued. "Then Lady Jane knelt down at the block and said aloud, 'Lord, into Thy hands I commend my spirit.' One blow from the ax, and it was over. The headsman picked up the severed head by the hair and cried out, 'So perish all the queen's enemies! Behold the head of a traitor!' The blood continued to pour out of her body in great quantity, and the crones pressed forward to sop it up. Later, when the curious had all gone away, it was my last duty to see her body laid beneath the altar pavement in the chapel of Saint Peter ad Vincula."

Lady Maud ceased her recital of horrors and squinted at me. "And there rests the nine-day queen, buried between Catherine Howard and your own mother, Anne Boleyn."

I began to weep. I wept for my former companion, at the reminder of the mother I scarcely remembered, and in fear for my own life. I now understood clearly that my sister would show no mercy to anyone she believed to be a threat to her throne, whether there was truth to such a threat or not.

CHAPTER 11

The Tower

Despite having summoned me to London, and despite my entreaties once I arrived, Queen Mary now refused to see me. Instead, members of the privy council came one by one to my frugal chambers at St. James's Palace. The questioning began. Everything depended upon my ability to summon my strength and to lie convincingly when I must.

What do you know of Thomas Wyatt?

"I know him to be the son of the poet of the same name. Thomas Wyatt the Elder was a favorite in the court of my father, King Henry the Eighth."

Did you conspire with Thomas Wyatt the Younger to overthrow Her Majesty, the queen?

"I would permit no conspiracy against Her Majesty, the queen, my beloved sister, to whom I have pledged my loyalty unto death."

Did Sir Thomas Wyatt inform you of his plans?

"I have had no contact whatsoever with Sir Thomas Wyatt, I swear it."

It is known that he wrote to you. Did you not receive his letters?

"I know of no letters." This was true; I knew of only one letter, not of *letters.*

Did you not reply to these letters?

"I can reply to no letters of which I have no knowledge."

Was it not your intent to become the wife of Edward Courtenay and then declare yourself queen?

"I have no wish to speak to the earl of Devon, let alone become his wife. As for declaring myself queen, I recognize but one queen, my beloved sister, Mary."

Thomas Wyatt was still alive, the examiners informed me, still held prisoner in the Tower. I knew that he would be tortured until he told the privy councillors the falsehood they wanted to hear: that I knew of and encouraged the plot against Mary. Wyatt had already implicated me. Now, his body stretched upon the rack, he would supply the details the councillors needed.

The questioning went on hour after hour, day after day. I was now twenty, five years older than I was when Sir Robert Tyrwhitt had questioned me at the time of Tom Seymour's arrest. Once again everything depended upon my wits, my skill at answering the questions in a way that would convince the interrogators of my innocence. Oddly enough, as my mind grew sharper, my body grew stronger. I was almost well again.

ON PALM SUNDAY, as I returned to my chambers from hearing Mass in the chapel royal, I found a half dozen guards waiting for me. I caught my breath.

"Why are you here?" I demanded.

"Ready yourself to leave, madam," said the captain.

The fierce expressions on the faces of the guards told me I was not being set free.

"Where, then?" I asked, dreading the answer.

"To the Tower, madam," replied the captain with a sneer.

"The Tower!" Had Thomas Wyatt persuaded them of my guilt? I was ready to swoon with fear. But I knew that I must not allow my terror to be seen. "No!" I cried. "By whose order?" I already knew the answer.

"By order of Her Majesty, the queen."

"Show me the order!"

The guard thrust the parchment before my face. I saw the signature, *Maria Regina.*

Thomas Wyatt had already been condemned to die. Was I to be next? *Please, God, no!*

The guards waited impatiently as Lady Cynthia and Lady Marian, looking stricken, packed my belongings. I signaled them, secretly, to be slow, to take as much time as possible, and I prayed silently for God's help. When my ladies could prolong their tasks no longer, I addressed the guards.

"Please bring me pen and paper, that I may send a message to my *sister,* the queen."

The guards exchanged glances. The lieutenant, a gawky youth, urged the captain to grant me my wish. "What can it hurt?" the boy whispered, and finally the other agreed.

"Make haste," grumbled the captain when the writing materials had been brought, "lest we miss the tide."

I knew well what he meant: We would travel by barge from the landing at St. James's, downriver, to the Tower. The Thames is subject to strong tides, which at certain times make passage through any of the twenty arches of London Bridge dangerous, if not impossible. Many boatmen and their passengers have gone to their watery graves by mistiming the passage of their craft. I gambled that these guards would not take such a risk, especially during the spring tide, when the water rose highest. In writing this letter, I might buy a little time— time for my sister to soften her heart and change her mind.

"I beg your indulgence, sirs," I said, sitting down at the writing table with parchment, inkhorn, and quill.

If only I could persuade Mary to allow me to meet with her! I knew that I could gaze, unblinking, into her eyes and lie without flinching. I would swear my unswerving loyalty to her and convince her of my innocence in any plot. Surely she could not bring herself to order my execution once she had looked into my face and been reminded that we two were daughters of the same mighty king!

Everything depended upon this letter. I chose each word with great care, while my guards muttered and shifted from foot to foot. Meanwhile, the ladies who were to be allowed to accompany me fell to weeping loudly, to the dismay of the young guard and the irritation of the elder.

When I had made every argument possible in my own favor, I added one more line to my letter: *I humbly crave but only one word of answer from yourself.* I signed it, *Your Highness's most faithful subject, that has been from the beginning and will be to my end, Elizabeth.* Then I drew a series of diagonal lines across the page below my signature so that no one else could fill in a postscript of his own devising.

I sealed the letter and rose from the table. "I am ready," I said. "Be so kind as to deliver this to Her Majesty, the queen."

The captain was plainly furious. "Too late, madam," he growled, red-faced. "The tide has already changed. We must wait six hours for it to change again."

"Then so it shall be," I said calmly. *Six hours—not much time, but enough.* "Perhaps, while we wait, the queen will see fit to answer, and we will have saved ourselves an unpleasant journey."

The hours dragged by, hours filled with foreboding. The Tower! My blood ran cold at the thought of it.

Then Lady Maud increased my dread with her report that the killings had begun. "The men who took part in the uprising against Queen Mary are being hanged in all parts of the city," she reported with evident relish. "Their bodies hang on gibbets, and their heads are impaled on posts above the city gates."

"How many?" asked my own Lady Marian.

"Forty-five at last count, and more to come, including Wyatt himself," replied Lady Maud. "They say the stench is quite dreadful." She held a pomander to her nose to make her point.

What of the "priest" who had brought me the message? I wondered. Was there still at large a man who knew that I had indeed received a letter from Thomas Wyatt, and that I had lied about it? May God forgive me, but I prayed that he was among those hanged and therefore unable to testify against me.

The six hours passed, but no messenger came. There was no reply from my sister, no letter granting me my request to speak with her.

"The time is at hand, madam," said the captain of the guard. "We leave within the hour. There can be no further delay."

I dressed in my most elegant gown and, shivering with fright, begged to be allowed to pray once more in the chapel royal before we left on this doleful journey. The captain consented, and I prayed fervently to the God of Protestants and Catholics alike to deliver me from this terrible ordeal.

The sky was dark and lowering, and a light rain fell. Bystanders crowded the riverbanks, craning to gape as the barge passed. I wondered if any in that silent crowd were sympathetic to me, or if they, like Mary, saw me as an enemy. The drizzle became a downpour as the barge approached the Water Gate. This gate was the one to which my mother had been brought, in this same manner, eighteen years earlier. I wept, thinking of how she had never left. I was following in the footsteps of many who had been accused of treason and whose last steps from freedom toward death had begun at this exact spot.

"Take me to another gate, any gate but this!" I cried. But the guards stared straight ahead, refusing to hear.

As I stepped from the barge, all strength drained from my legs, which gave way under me. Overcome by terror, I collapsed onto the stone steps, which were wet from the lapping river. I lay crumpled in the rain, unable to go another step. The warders of the Tower sent to meet me stared down at me. I gazed up at them, searching for a sympathetic face. I felt utterly without hope.

Then one, followed by another, abruptly stepped out of the formation, cried, "God preserve Your Grace!" and knelt before me. Immediately others of the warders seized me roughly, set me upon my feet, and ordered me to enter the Tower.

We—my ladies and I—found ourselves shut up in a dank stone chamber on the first floor of the Bell Tower. In the corner lay a rude pallet for sleeping. Under the arched windows were stone seats. The room held nothing else.

As I stood shivering in my sodden, mud-splattered gown and surveyed my rude quarters, I realized that I must summon my will and immediately command the respect of my warders. I must not show any hint of fear or weakness. "What arrangements have been made for me?" I demanded imperiously of the warder with the great ring of keys clanking at his side.

"Ye'll stay here, madam," said the warder.

"Am I to have no place to take bodily exercise?" I insisted. "Am I to eat the food of common prisoners? I am sister to the queen!"

The warder left, mumbling his intent to do everything possible to please me. As soon as he was gone, I slumped down on one of the stone benches and burst into tears.

My orders were actually obeyed. That same day a tester bed with a mattress of fair quality was moved into the chamber. A day later ten servants were assigned to prepare and serve my meals. And within the week I was granted permission to walk twice each day along the lead, the narrow walkway on top of the wall from the Bell Tower to Beauchamp Tower. From this vantage point I could look out over the parapet toward the spire of St. Paul's. I purposely kept my back to the view in another direction: the Tower Green, where my mother had been executed, where Lady Jane Grey had died, and where, I prayed, my life would not also end.

The days succeeded one another in a dull, orderly manner. I prayed, read, took my walks on the lead, and passed the time with needlework. Meals were brought to my chamber, and every dish was searched before it was served, lest some message be smuggled to me in a meat pie or a manchet! My temper was worn thin, and I often spoke sharply to my ladies and then regretted it. They were with me of their own free will and could have left me if they wished.

In April I learned that Sir Thomas Wyatt had been executed in the horrible manner reserved for traitors: After his beheading on Tower Hill, his head was taken to be displayed near Hyde Park. Then his corpse was parboiled, cut into four parts, and each part displayed in a different quarter of the city as a warning.

There were other prisoners whose fate I sometimes wondered about—most especially Robin Dudley, who had been arrested after his father's failed attempt to capture Mary. Where was he now? Alive or dead? Was he also a prisoner in this Tower? No one told me, and I did not want to put myself in more danger by asking.

WEEKS PASSED. Mary could not have forgotten me, although I did feel she had utterly abandoned me. I knew that the members of the privy council did not believe in my innocence. If it had been up to them—Sir William Paget and the earl of Arundel—I would have been put to death immediately. I was sure they would try to convince the queen that I was not to be trusted, that her crown was not secure as long as I was alive. I could imagine my sister's endless debates with her councillors:

What shall we do with Elizabeth?

We cannot execute her—that would cause an enormous outcry, a rebellion.

We cannot keep her locked up in the Tower forever—that, too, would likely cause an uprising.

And we surely cannot set her free—she is too dangerous for that!

If we brought her to court, we could watch her closely—but having her at court is an offense to the queen!

So, what shall we do with Elizabeth?

Every night as I lay down in my barren chamber, I thanked God for granting me one more day. Every morning I awoke thinking that this day might be my last.

ON THE NINETEENTH of May in 1554, the anniversary of my mother's execution and three long months after I had been taken to London from Ashridge, a detachment of guards arrived at the Tower and ordered me to prepare to leave. I stood stock-still, as if made of wood.

"Where are you taking me?" I asked.

"It is not permitted to inform the prisoner."

So, I was still a prisoner. But I was not to be executed—at least not yet. A condemned prisoner is sent a priest to hear a last confession, and there was no priest.

Down to the Water Gate we went, my footsteps dragging. I was grateful to be alive, but still very frightened. I had no idea what lay ahead.

CHAPTER 12

Elizabeth, Prisoner

I refused to look back at the Tower as the oarsmen bent to their task and the unpainted wooden boat moved upstream with the tide, passing under the arches of London Bridge. No one on the banks paused for a second look. Eventually we made for the landing at Richmond Palace.

"Why are we stopping here?" I asked one of the guards, who bore a livid scar from ear to chin.

"Orders of Her Majesty, the queen" was the gruff reply, a reply that told me nothing.

Once inside the palace I was led to a bare chamber. The door was quickly shut and locked from the outside, and I was entirely alone.

"Where are my ladies?" I cried, pounding on the wooden door. "My servants?"

"You are permitted to speak to no one," said the guard through a small opening in the door covered by an iron grille.

I paced fretfully, first the length of the small chamber and then the breadth. The single window was too high for me to see anything but a patch of blue sky. Gradually the sky grew dark.

Sometime later the guard returned with a bowl of rank-smelling mutton stew and a pewter tankard of ale, which he set just inside the door. I could not bear to touch either one. The sky faded to inky blackness.

All night I lay awake on a pallet on the floor, with only a thin coverlet. Terrified, I was certain I had been brought here so that my death could be accomplished in secrecy, to prevent an outcry from my friends and whatever supporters I might have. Wyatt was dead, along with others involved in the rebellion. But were there some still alive who wished me to be their queen? Would they have the courage to risk everything to show their support?

The hours passed, but no soldiers arrived to drag me off to one of the dungeons in the depths of the palace. When the patch of sky at my window grew light again, the captain of the guards, the one with the scar, informed me that we were ready "to continue the journey."

I decided I would not give him the satisfaction of my asking any more questions. There was no sign of my ladies-in-waiting. They had all been dismissed. Surrounded by the blank faces and foul breath of the men sent to guard me, I would have welcomed even Lady Maud for companionship.

Fear cloaked me like a worn-out garment as I stepped once more onto the barge. We proceeded upriver, attracting no notice, until we reached Windsor Castle. The guards took me not to the great castle itself but to a small house near St. George's Chapel, where my father's bones lay buried. There I was again locked away and passed another tormented night, listening for the tramp of feet, the click of a key in the lock, a stealthy executioner come to take my life. But another dawn broke, and miraculously I was still alive.

Not long after sunrise I was led out to the courtyard, where a rude litter waited. Also waiting was Sir Henry Bedingfield, a member of the queen's privy council. Bewhiskered and bejowled, Sir Henry presented himself to me upon his knees. "The queen has made me responsible for your safety and comfort," he said, hands clasped and jowls aquiver. "I beg you, madam, regard me not as jailer but as an officer in your service."

"Good Lord, deliver me from such officers," I snapped. I climbed into the litter, and the journey continued, with Bedingfield riding by my side. We had turned away from the river and made our way through the green and flowering countryside. We seemed to be headed north and west, possibly toward Oxfordshire.

Although every effort had been made to conceal

the fact that I was a person of any importance, word had somehow spread that King Henry's younger daughter was traveling through the villages and hamlets. Signaled by the ringing of church bells, people all along our route turned out to welcome me. Little boys rode their fathers' shoulders and cheered, "God save you, Princess!" Mothers pushed their daughters forward to present me with sweetmeats and nosegays. So many gifts were heaped upon my litter that scarcely any room was left for me.

This spontaneous outpouring of goodwill and affection lifted my spirits. For the first time in months, I felt hopeful. I did have supporters, then—the simple folk of the countryside. All this wild enthusiasm made Bedingfield impatient and uneasy. He glowered at the cheering farmers and yeomen and goodwives but made no move to stop them.

Waving and laughing, I called out, "Good people, I beg you, keep these wondrous cakes for your own enjoyment!" But that didn't stop them. I was their own Princess Elizabeth, daughter of their beloved King Henry, and they seemed determined to show their love for me. *It is a great thing to be loved,* I thought; *far better than to be feared.*

We halted for the night at the village of Rycote, where the lord of the manor entertained me lavishly under Bedingfield's disapproving eye. It had been a long time since I'd enjoyed such a feast. As we prepared to leave the next morning, I thanked the baron for his hospitality.

"Bear in mind, madam," said the baron quietly as he bowed over my hand, "that you have many supporters who will gladly serve you as queen."

I smiled and nodded and hurried away. Fortunately, Henry Bedingfield was then occupied with our horses and heard nothing. But my host's generous comment stayed with me as we rode on. I had the love of the common people, and I had the loyalty of some of the nobility who would one day serve me. But I could not rule if I did not survive. I saw plainly that henceforward my principal task was to stay alive—to wait and to watch.

AT LAST the journey ended at Woodstock Palace. Long ago a favorite hunting lodge of Norman kings, it was now reduced to a dilapidated pile of crumbling stone and shattered casement windows in the midst of a marsh reeking of decay.

"I am to stay here?" I cried. "Surely not!"

One look was sufficient to convince even Sir Henry that the old palace to which I'd been banished was not fit even for a jail. He decided that I must make my residence in the gatehouse. It took less time to inspect my quarters than it does now to describe them: for my use, a single chamber with mildewed walls and a rather curiously carved roof, to be shared with my maidservants; a chapel; a second chamber for Sir Henry and our menservants; and a third for my guards. This was where I would pass my days and nights, for I knew not how long.

Bedingfield's first act was to read me the rules, as set forth by Queen Mary: "The lady Elizabeth is forbidden to walk in the garden without an officer present. She is forbidden to receive any kind of message, letter, or gift from anyone at all."

"Books?" I interrupted. "Surely I am permitted any books I choose."

Bedingfield thumbed through the queen's rules. "Only such books as specified," he said. "Any special requests are to be made to me, and I will forward them to the privy council, who will consider the matter."

"This is outrageous, sir!" I exclaimed.

Sir Henry dropped to his knees. "Begging your pardon, madam, but I can make no exceptions, nor can I make any decisions on my own." He seemed genuinely sorry.

"Very well. Might I then also have a Bible in English?"

"I shall write to the council, madam."

After a long delay, back came the reply: The queen forbids all of her subjects (no exceptions) to read the Bible in any language but Latin. I could of course read Latin as easily as English, but it was the principle of the thing, and her refusal put me in a foul temper.

Worse even than the rude quarters was the confinement. There was nowhere to go, nothing to do, no one to talk to but the tongue-tied maidservants.

When I saw how life would be at Woodstock, I determined to write a letter to the queen. My request for writing supplies had first to be sent to the privy council, since Bedingfield was forbidden to allow me the use of his parchment, quill, and ink. The councillors dithered and fretted, suspicious that I might be plotting to incite a rebellion. Assured that I wished only to write to my sister, they relented. The materials were sent—but only in small quantity—and I composed a message, repeating to Queen Mary my declarations of loyalty and begging with all my heart for her leniency.

This turned out to be a poor idea, or perhaps it was poorly executed. Whatever the cause, my message was poorly received. In reply I got a sharp rebuke from the queen: *Our pleasure is not to be anymore molested with such letters.*

I read the queen's message and wept. I shouted at Sir Henry and flung the inkhorn with what was left of the ink against the wall. Then I collapsed in sobs, realizing that, added to my misery, I had just wasted one of my precious resources.

Never has time crept so slowly! An elderly priest came from the village each day to say Mass in the musty chapel. My dinner was brought in midmorning, most often a meat pasty or a stew made of wild game, and a tankard of ale. The women who served me were dull. After dinner I had nothing but stitch after stitch after stitch of needlework to mark the passage of the long afternoon hours. Supper arrived, the priest returned for vespers, followed by an evening of reading and more stitchery, until my eyes ached and my head throbbed, and I longed for sleep.

I thought often of Kat and wondered how she fared.

I missed the visits from Sir William Cecil, who had once kept me informed of events in the court's inner circle. Bedingfield offered no companionship—I avoided him and, I'm certain, he avoided *me*.

Even getting out of bed each morning took effort. To cheer myself I sometimes recalled the goodwill and affection of the common people who had turned out to cheer me, and the words of my host at Rycote. I knew that I had supporters out there, although I could not guess their strength. There must have been sufficient numbers to convince my sister that they—and I— were a danger to her, or she would not have kept me prisoner. I also knew that unless these supporters somehow did manage to organize a successful rebellion without my participation, my life might well continue this way until my sister died.

And if a rebel leader did succeed in asking for my help, what then? I could not agree. The risk of failure was too great—and it was my head that would be lost.

One day, when I felt sure that I would waste away my entire life within the moldering walls of this wretched place, I scratched my despair upon the pane of a window, using the diamond in my ring:

> Much suspected, by me
> Nothing proved can be
> Quoth Elizabeth, prisoner

CHAPTER 13

Lady Bess

I'm certain that I was the unhappiest woman in all of England. Day after day throughout the summer, the rain fell ceaselessly, the marshes reeked, and my quarters stank to high heaven. Under other circumstances I would have packed up and moved to another residence so that this one could be thoroughly cleansed. At the very least I wished the filthy rushes on the floor could be swept out and the mattresses aired. Even with a pomander handy to my nose, the stench was unbearable.

Then, in August, Bedingfield informed me that the privy council was sending me a lady to be my companion. "Her name is Elizabeth Sands," said Sir Henry. "She has been a member of the queen's court for some years, and Her Majesty thinks highly of her."

"I assume that she is another spy for the queen," I replied sullenly, "although I cannot imagine what she will find to spy upon in this woeful place."

Within a fortnight my new companion arrived, a short, plump woman with a heart-shaped faced. "Was your journey a pleasant one?" I asked, not caring whether it was or not.

"A pleasant journey to a place wretched in every way but my lady's company," she said, regarding the quarters we would share.

"Why have you come here?" I asked.

"Because the queen fears that you are lonely."

I laughed bitterly.

But Lady Bess, as I called her, quickly eased my suspicions and won me over. I found her both merry at heart and serious of mind. She also proved to be a marvelous gossip, as good as Kat ever was.

"You know of the queen's marriage?" Bess asked on her second day, as we each bent over a new piece of needlework.

"I knew only that she planned to marry. Has the wedding taken place, then?"

"It has. On the twenty-fifth of July, on the Feast of Saint James, patron saint of Spain, Queen Mary married King Philip."

"And now it is *King* Philip? When last I heard he was only a prince."

"On the night before the wedding, word came that Philip's father had made him king of Naples. The announcement was read out, and all the nobles rushed to kiss his hands. Mary never stopped grinning."

"You were there? You saw?"

Bess nodded, smiling wickedly. "I was there. I saw."

"Then tell me!" I half ordered, half pleaded, starved as I was for conversation of any sort.

For the next hour Bess described in considerable detail the scene at Winchester Cathedral—the cloth of gold hung on the walls of the church, the five bishops all in purple, Philip wearing a white doublet and breeches and draped with the mantle Mary had sent him as a gift.

Bess missed no particular: "There were two dozen large buttons on each of his sleeves, each button made of four large pearls."

"And my sister?"

"Black velvet covered all over with jewels. Her mantle matched the king's, cloth of gold trimmed with crimson velvet. She was followed by fifty gentlewomen, all in cloth of silver. The solemnities went on for hours, and the queen never took her eyes off the blessed sacrament."

"A saintly woman," I murmured, although in fact I thought her anything but saintly. No saint treated a sister as hatefully as Mary treated me.

Bess looked at me sharply. "So it is said."

"And the banquet?" I pressed. "You were present for that as well?"

"I was, madam."

"And? Tell me of it!"

Bess squinted at her needle and slipped a silken thread through the narrow eye. "If I tell you everything today, dear lady Elizabeth, there will be nothing left to tell tomorrow."

That night I invited Bess to sleep in my bed, rather than on the pallet provided for her on the damp floor. I slept soundly for the first time in many months. The next afternoon, faithful to her word, she continued her description of the wedding feast.

"I thought it would never end. The royal bride and groom were seated, but the guests ate standing up. There were four courses, each with thirty dishes. As each dish was presented, trumpets blew a fanfare and everyone bowed low. It lasted for hours. And it was very impressive—more gold and silver plate than I have ever seen in one place.

"But I did notice two things: The queen's chair was more elaborate than King Philip's, and she was served on gold plate while Philip was served on silver. If I noticed the difference, you can be sure the Spanish nobility did as well. They think we are uncouth barbarians as it is."

"Few English think well of the Spaniards," I said. "Now tell me about the dancing."

"Tomorrow," said Bess, and I could not extract another word from her on the subject.

Then a servant arrived with our supper, a fresh fish sent to us by a neighboring farmer. My appetite returned, I savored that fish more than I would have any wedding banquet.

THE NEXT AFTERNOON, the first fair day we'd had in weeks, I begged Sir Henry to allow me and my companion to walk together in the garden. He refused, and my mood turned sour.

Lady Bess brushed aside my disappointment. "The smell out there is at least as bad as the smell in here," she said. "Take up your needlework, Lady Elizabeth, and I shall tell you about the wedding dance."

I resigned myself to the piece of linen I'd been working with an elaborate chain-stitch design. "Go on," I said, eager for every detail.

"It was not a great success," said Bess. "The English noblemen and their ladies were not acquainted with the dances of the Spaniards, and the other way around. Dancing together proved even more difficult than conversing together, which was almost impossible. The Spaniards spoke no English, the English spoke no Spanish. The king and queen danced together in the German style, which they both seemed to know, but I can say in all confidence that the queen far outshone her husband in this."

"Here I am, shut up in a stinking gatehouse, while my sister dances!" I cried, and flung my needlework as far as I could. For my companion's sake I collected my-self. Bess skillfully changed the subject, and I asked for no more details that day.

"HAVE YOU NEWS of the wedding night?" I asked when I felt ready for another installment.

"I was not present, madam," she said with a droll wink. "But just before I left to come to you, I heard this: At about nine o'clock, the last of the guests left the wedding feast, and the king and queen went to their separate apartments to dine alone. Later they met again in the bedchamber that had been prepared for them, the marital bed blessed by the chancellor. The next morning Philip's gentlemen came knocking at the door of the chamber, following the Spanish custom of greet-ing the king in bed on the morning after the marriage. But Mary's ladies knew nothing of this custom and barred the door. 'Imagine,' one said later to me, 'calling on a bride the morning after her wedding night! It is indecent!' "

"Pity the queen," I snorted, not bothering to sup-press an unkind laugh. "It must all have been a shock to her."

Once we'd exhausted the particulars of my sister's wedding, we played games of words that required prodigious feats of memory. Bess was no scholar, and my attempts to interest her in the Latin poets bore no fruit. Likewise, she was a poor musician, whose fingers turned to thumbs on the lute strings. She loved horses and hunting as much as I did, but that was of no use since we were not allowed any outdoor activities. And so we stitched and talked, and—upon occasion—even laughed out loud. It had not taken long for me to learn to trust Bess and to value her companionship.

My twenty-first birthday passed unremarked by any but Lady Bess. We enjoyed a string of golden September days before the nights turned cold and the rains began again. The winds whipped around (and through) the gatehouse, giving a foretaste of how unpleasant our winter was to be.

The roof leaked badly, and many of the window-panes were broken. I importuned Bedingfield to urge the privy council to repair the building, lest we all freeze in the coming months. The queen, whom I imag-ined swept away with wedded bliss in the arms of her new husband, can scarcely have given a thought to the poor sister whose life was draining away like water through a sieve.

Bess and I were careful what we said to each other during the day, when there was the danger of being overheard. But at night, once the bed curtains were drawn and we were certain the maidservants, who slept on pallets on the floor, were fast asleep, we confided in each other, sometimes whispering for hours.

"The farmer who sent you the fresh fish has been forbidden to return," Lady Bess murmured softly one night. "He is said to be one of your strongest supporters, and Sir Henry fears that he may be part of a plot to lead a rising in your behalf."

I hushed her. To make sure the maids were truly asleep, I climbed out of bed and relieved myself in the chamber pot. When that failed to awaken them, I crept back under the worn coverlet and we continued the conversation. "You must understand, Bess, that I will take part in no rebellion," I said. "It is far too dangerous. I have made that clear to everyone."

"Perhaps there is no need for a rebellion," said Bess. "Sooner or later, you will inherit the throne from Mary. I pray that it is sooner, rather than later."

"Not if the queen has a child. Then he will become king, and his children will succeed him, and I will die here alone and forgotten," I said, my voice breaking.

Bess propped herself on an elbow. "Mary is thirty-eight, surely too old to bear a child."

"It is not impossible," I said, thinking of Queen Catherine, who was thirty-six when she birthed Tom Seymour's child.

"She has not the health for it," Bess insisted. "You need only be patient. And prudent."

Thus, even though it was perhaps neither prudent nor wise, we had our nightly conversations behind the bed curtains. One or the other of us would use the chamber pot to make sure the servants were sleeping. Then Bess would prompt me, "When you are queen, what shall you do?" Guided by her astute questions, I began to envision my future.

"I will restore the Protestant Church and make it the official church of England, as my father intended, but I will not punish those who are Catholic or force them to give up their faith." Another time I said, "I will have a council made up of the ablest and wisest men in the kingdom. Sir William Cecil, for instance. And," I added, "I shall never marry. I shall never relinquish control of my life to a husband."

I SHOULD HAVE known that Lady Bess would be sent away. Sir Henry disliked her, probably simply because I liked her very much. I'm sure it was by his doing that Mary ordered her dismissal, calling my friend "a person of evil opinion, not fit to remain about our sister." But Bess had once been a lady of her court! Had our secret conversations been overheard after all?

"You will be a magnificent queen one day," Bess whispered as we embraced one last time. I watched her ride away as tears streamed unchecked down my face. I was alone again.

Sometimes, late at night, in the weeks after she'd gone, I thought of Lady Bess's parting words and the hope sustained me: *I shall be the next queen of England. I shall be the next to wear the crown.*

But on the twenty-seventh of November that hope was shattered. A messenger arrived to tell us the news, proclaimed throughout the kingdom, that the queen was with child. Resentfully, I began at once to stitch a set of tiny garments of the finest white linen with edgings of red silk, fit for the newborn prince or princess.

The winter passed wretchedly. I continued to make a show of worshiping as a Catholic, hearing Mass twice each day. But I was often so cold that my fingers were too stiff to finger the beads of my rosary or to stitch the little gowns and caps for the royal babe who would one day take my place as heir to the throne. Despair was my companion, night and day.

CHAPTER 14

Waiting

Somehow I endured the bleak and lonely winter. Then, in the spring of 1555, Queen Mary ordered Sir Henry to bring me to Hampton Court. She had retired there on the fourth of April to await the birth of her babe. By tradition my presence was required at the queen's labor and delivery of the heir who would replace me in the line of succession. I didn't relish this duty nor, I am sure, did my sister. Still, I was immensely relieved to leave Woodstock.

As I made the long journey to Hampton Court, I understood that my future was grim. With the birth of Mary's child, my hope of becoming queen would end. And as long as I was alive, I would remain a threat to the heir who was about to take my place. I pondered the choices the queen might make if she continued to distrust me. She could send me back to prison, at Woodstock or some other godforsaken place, and leave me there until her heir might one day decide to free me, when I was old and toothless. She could force me to marry some foreign nobleman and move to the Continent as an alternative to imprisonment. Or she could find a pretext of treason and condemn me to death.

Now, instead of relishing the crowds that would turn out to cheer me, I feared that they'd give the queen the excuse she needed to send me to the Tower and then to the block. I begged Sir Henry to keep my movements secret, which he was pleased to do. There were no crowds, and no visits to the country manors of sympathetic noblemen.

When I arrived at Hampton Court in mid-April, I learned that Queen Mary had ordered me kept in seclusion, with just four ladies and four gentlemen to attend me. I was still a prisoner, forbidden to leave, forbidden to receive visitors. And I was not permitted to speak to the queen.

Hampton Court, with a thousand rooms, was crowded. Many had assembled, for the birth: physicians and midwives to attend the queen, wet nurses and rockers for the babe, noblemen and gentlewomen, who were simply to be present for the great event, and the servants of all. There was an air of excited anticipation as the wait began.

Each morning I arose and made my way to the chapel royal for Mass, making sure that I was observed by the queen's favorites, Lady Susan Clarencieux and Lady Jane Dormer, who would certainly report to her on my piety—or lack of it. Then I returned to my apartments to await the summons to the queen's bedchamber when her labor began.

I was restless, and I asked for and received permission to walk in the gardens with my ladies—and my guards. With so many people about, the guards soon grew lax, and it was on one of these walks that I encountered a stranger who begged leave to speak with me. He was, he claimed, a friend of my cousin, Catherine Knollys. A large hat shielded his face.

Smiling, I turned to my ladies. "The son of my former governess," I lied boldly. "We have not seen each other since we shared a tutor." I took the stranger's arm and we strolled on, feigning an animated conversation about an invented childhood, until my ladies lost interest. "Pray, continue," I said.

Having been locked away at Woodstock, I knew nothing of what this stranger now told me. With growing horror I listened as he described how Queen Mary had decided to rid the kingdom of those who refused to follow the Catholic faith—heretics, she claimed, who committed treason against God. Most Protestants of the nobility, such as my cousin and her husband and child, as well as the most outspoken Protestant leaders, had already fled to the Continent. The queen was determined to make examples of those who elected to stay and had issued the following order: *Give up your evil and corrupt beliefs, or be burned alive.*

"The bravest have chosen death, and the burning of the heretics began during the past winter," the stranger said in a low voice. "Many have already died."

"Who are you?" I asked finally.

"Not one of the brave," said the stranger. "When I have finished, you must forget that you have seen me."

My ladies were staring, having detected a change in his demeanor. It would not be long until even the lazy guards noticed something amiss. "Go on," I urged, "but quickly!"

"Among the first of the heretics to die," said my informant, "was John Hooper, bishop of Gloucester. Because of the dampness in the air and the blustery winds, he burned for an hour until death released him."

"You witnessed it all?" I asked.

"I did. The bishop was placed on a high stool so that everyone might see him. He was first secured to the stake that would support him and branches piled around the stool. When the torch was put to the branches, we expected him to be consumed at once by flames. But the branches were of green wood, and a sharp gust of wind blew out the feeble flames before they had done more than singe his robe."

"Perhaps it was a sign," I suggested, "that he was to be spared."

"Perhaps," said the witness, "but the queen's agents were determined to carry out their duty. They added more branches, with no greater success. In a third attempt bags of gunpowder were tied to his legs. The powder was to explode and kill him outright, so that he would not have to suffer the horrible pain. It was thought to be merciful."

I reached for my handkerchief and pressed it to my lips. "Finish this dreadful tale, I beg you," I said.

My informant drew a wavering breath. "The wind blew away the powder. It helped him not at all. We heard him cry out, 'Lord Jesus, have mercy upon me!' His cries continued, even as the flames licked at his throat, until, finally he could no longer utter a sound. At last he bowed his head and died."

"God have mercy on us all!" I exclaimed.

"Take care, take care!" warned the witness, and before I could say more, he melted into the shadows.

What kind of monster is she? I wondered as I tried to recover my composure. Queen Mary herself would show no mercy to those who did not believe as she did. Although she was, for the moment, ignoring me, the cruelty of the queen to those she called heretics made me very afraid.

ALL WAS IN READINESS for the birth, yet nothing happened. At the end of April, a rumor spread that the queen had given birth to a son. Those who kept watch outside her privy chamber knew this was not true, but the rumor flew unchecked, and great celebrations were reported in the streets of London. I can only imagine the disappointment and dismay that followed when the rumor proved false.

Early in May the queen's physicians, in consultation with her astrologers, announced that there had been a miscalculation. Now, instead of the first week of May, the babe was expected to arrive either late in the month or after the full moon on the fourth or fifth of June.

Although I repeatedly requested an interview with my sister, she refused to see me. Everyone was as restless as I. There was no court life—no feasting, no dancing, no masques or music—only the endless waiting.

I wondered how King Philip was passing this fretful time. I had glimpsed him only briefly, as he made his way through the queen's presence chamber to visit her. It occurred to me that if I could somehow make his acquaintance, I might persuade him to intervene on my behalf with my sister. I would watch for an opportunity.

To break the tedium, one afternoon late in May, I went walking in the royal park with two of my hardier ladies, ignoring the rain that fell endlessly. The guards who were supposed to escort me on these walks found an excuse to seek shelter. Approaching from the opposite direction, I observed, was a grandly attired nobleman, accompanied by several disgruntled-looking gentlemen. I recognized my brother-in-law. As he drew near I made a hurried decision and dropped to my knees in the mud.

"Your Grace," I began, addressing him in Spanish. He halted and looked at me closely. Continuing in Latin, for I was not fluent in Spanish, I said, "I am Elizabeth, sister to Her Majesty, the queen."

Immediately he raised me up and replied, "It is with the greatest of pleasure that I make your acquaintance." Philip bowed over my hand and kissed it.

We conversed for some little time, and I asked after the health of his wife. "The queen is well, madam," he answered, although I doubted that. "And you, my lady Elizabeth? Your accommodations are quite comfortable?"

"Entirely satisfactory, Your Majesty," I lied, and then told another lie: "My greatest pleasure is in being here to serve my dear sister at this most happy event. But you would do me a great kindness," I added with a winsome smile, "if you would assure Her Majesty, the queen, of my love and loyalty and arrange for me to meet with her. She trusts me not."

The king gave me a long and searching look before he replied. "I will do this for you, dear lady Elizabeth," he said with another bow.

I knew that my gown was muddied and my hair was damp and unruly, but I also saw from his pleased expression that the king thought well of me. I was aware of the risk: I desired his admiration, but I must take great care not to arouse the queen's jealousy.

I began to watch for other opportunities for such accidental meetings, and I believe Philip was also contriving such encounters. "My lady Elizabeth," he would say as we happened to meet in the gardens, "do you not find the English weather oppressive?" And I would say something like, "I trust that God continues to bless our queen with good health," and then, in my most engaging manner, I would remind him once again to arrange for me to speak with the queen. I felt quite sure that I could eventually persuade Philip to do what I wished.

At long last, late one evening toward the end of May, Lady Susan Clarencieux appeared at my chambers. "Her Majesty, the queen, requests your company," she said, her dislike of me evident in her voice and demeanor.

Philip must have finally intervened with the queen on my behalf. At last I would have an opportunity to meet with my sister and to swear again my loyalty. While Lady Susan scowled, my maids laced me into a white petticoat and a black velvet gown and clasped a gold cross about my neck. Then, with a half dozen attendants carrying smoking torches, I was led through the garden and into another part of the palace through a side door.

"Why are we going to visit Her Majesty by this way?" I asked uneasily as we mounted a dark and narrow stairway. There was no reply. Immediately I suspected a trap. But we kept walking through the gloomy back halls of the palace.

At last we passed through the queen's presence chamber and into her privy chamber. My mouth was dry with apprehension. As I knelt three times, I observed with a shock how much Mary had aged in sixteen months, how weary she looked. And how thin! Instead of having the roundness of pregnancy, her body appeared gaunt. My mind raced. *Is she truly expecting a child?* It had not occurred to me before that perhaps she was not. Behind Mary the doors to the bedchamber stood open. Through them I could see the great carved cradle of estate, ready and waiting for the royal babe. *What if there is to be no royal babe?* There was no time to think of this now as the queen sat glaring at me.

Clasping my hands to keep them from trembling, I dropped to my knees and cried passionately, "God preserve Your Majesty! I am as true a subject as any, no matter what has been said of me!"

But the very sight of me seemed to anger the queen. "You!" she stormed. "You lie to us! You are no more a believer in the one true faith than ever you were, and yet you persist in this pretense!"

"But, Your Majesty," I said through honest tears, "I have done all that you asked of me. All I ask is that you have a good opinion of me."

"We have no opinion whatsoever of you, Elizabeth," she said sharply.

With a wave of her hand, I was dismissed, and I was escorted back to my chambers. The long-awaited audience had been a failure. There may have been no trap that night, but neither was there reconciliation. I felt sick at heart.

Thereafter I kept my distance from King Philip; he had done nothing to improve the queen's opinion of me, and it was dangerous to continue what might be seen as a flirtation. May gave way to June, and still there was no child. By now I was sure that the queen was not pregnant. *Did she miscarry in the early months? Or has she perhaps imagined it all?* Of course, there was no one to whom I could speak aloud—or even whisper—of this.

THE RAIN was relentless, which made the wait for a birth—or the denial of one—almost insupportable. The air seemed heavy with frustration and misplaced hope. The throngs crowded into even so vast a palace as Hampton Court turned it into a place as foul-smelling as Woodstock. And I chafed at the knowledge that Mary despised me but nevertheless insisted upon keeping me there. I could do nothing.

Gossip was rampant. I heard whispers in the halls and courtyards that if Mary did not survive childbirth, King Philip would have me as his wife. The thought made me shudder.

I heard it whispered that the queen's child could not be born until every heretic had been burned, and that Mary herself had said it. It seemed that she must believe such a thing, for the burnings continued at a frightening rate. I tried to shut my ears to the horrifying reports and despaired that the nightmare would ever end.

CHAPTER 15

King Philip's Departure

Late in July the physicians, midwives, astrologers, ladies-in-waiting, and Mary herself finally admitted that the queen was not pregnant. No official announcement was made. We were simply told that the queen and her court were moving to Oatlands, a great country house in Surrey, so that Hampton Court could be cleansed.

I was ordered to move along with the rest of the queen's attendants. I was still not free. Without the birth of an heir to take my place in the succession, I was once again next in line for the throne. But I was still very uneasy about my future. What would the queen do with me now? Send me back to Woodstock? Or worse?

After we were settled at Oatlands and the queen had begun to resume her royal duties, I received a visit from one of her chaplains, Father Francis. The old priest took such a long route to arrive at the heart of his mission that for some time I had no idea why he was sitting in my apartments. I offered him drink, which he accepted. Then I offered him bread and meat, and he accepted those. When he had finished eating and drinking, he sighed contentedly and went on to talk about gardening, in which he had a deep interest. Thinking that perhaps the chaplain had been sent to trap me in a heresy, I was on my guard.

"The continuing rain is taking its toll," he said.

"It is indeed," I agreed. *But why are you here?*

"My garden is in ruins."

"I am sorry to hear that." *Get to the point!*

"In King Henry's time," he went on, "I was in charge of the herbarium at a monastery. Before it was closed."

"A rewarding vocation, I should think." *What a waste of my time!*

As the conversation rambled on about the priest's failed attempts to cultivate a particular kind of hyssop, my impatience at last overcame me, and I begged him to reveal the purpose of his visit.

Father Francis looked surprised. "Why, to discuss with you the prospect of a husband, Lady Elizabeth. This is a matter of great concern to Her Majesty, the queen."

So it was matrimony he had come to discuss, not

heresy! "Then let us proceed," I said. It seemed prudent to hear him out.

"It has been proposed that you marry Don Carlos, the son of King Philip by his first wife, Maria of Portugal, who died in childbirth."

I stared at Father Francis in disbelief. "Don Carlos is but a child," I said.

"He is nine years old," said the priest, nodding. "You would become betrothed as soon as it can be arranged, but you would not marry until the prince has reached the age of sixteen." Father Francis must have seen the look of dismay on my face, for he added hastily, "Or perhaps earlier, if madam wishes."

"The boy is said to suffer from certain difficulties," I said, choosing my words carefully. In fact, it was common knowledge that the king's son showed signs of madness and had to be kept shut away.

"Many things can happen in six years," Father Francis said soothingly. "The lad may outgrow the difficulties."

"Please deliver this message to the queen, and to the king as well," I said flatly. "I will not marry Don Carlos."

"Ah, dear, dear, dear," sighed the priest, peering into his empty tankard.

I knew, even as I uttered the words, that defiance of the queen was a highly dangerous move. But I was prepared to risk another imprisonment rather than enter into such a vile marriage. Would I risk death as well? *If I must,* I thought. Greatly agitated, I rose, but the chaplain seemed not to have noticed my gesture of dismissal. I calmed myself and called for more ale to be brought. Perhaps I could learn more from this thirsty priest.

"Are there other candidates?" I asked as he contentedly laced his fingers across his ample belly.

"There has been a mention of a German prince, Margrave of Baden, but that match was dismissed. The prince is Protestant, and naturally Her Majesty, the queen, insists that you marry a Catholic."

"Naturally." I was tempted to add, *And I insist that I marry no one at all!* But I held my tongue.

My marriage to the prince, or to any foreign Catholic nobleman, would have made Queen Mary's life much easier. In one stroke she would send me out of the country and away from the Protestant supporters, who, I believed, wanted me as their queen. I prayed that those friends were still supporting me, still willing to bide their time.

"And another gentleman once came to claim you—you know of that?" Father Francis continued.

"I do not."

"Emmanuel Philibert, duke of Savoy. The duke is a cousin of the king's. When he heard that King Philip was kindly disposed toward him as your future husband, he was so pleased that he traveled all the way to London to 'pluck the fruit'—his very words, I am told. No one had advised the king and queen that he was coming, and no one had informed the duke that you were indisposed to see visitors at Woodstock."

"I was not indisposed. I was imprisoned there," I retorted.

"Yes . . . well. Whatever the situation. At any rate, he passed a month at Somerset House—"

"The duke stayed at my house?" I asked, incredulous. "Without my leave?"

"At the invitation of Their Majesties," the priest said smoothly. "But after a month of waiting, with no reward, the duke returned to Savoy. I understand that he went away quite disappointed."

"No doubt," I replied.

The priest's tankard stood empty once more, and when I made no move to fill it a third time, he leaned forward and patted my hand. "Be of good cheer, madam," he said. "I am certain that we shall be able to find you a fine husband."

I had nearly bitten through my tongue by the time he left me with his blessing!

WEEKS LATER the court prepared to move again, this time to Greenwich Palace. Philip had recently been made king of the Netherlands by his aging father, Emperor Charles V, and he was soon to depart for Flanders, to acquaint himself with his new kingdom.

The royal couple traveled through London in an open litter, so that Mary's subjects could see for themselves that their queen and her consort were alive and well. I was sent by water, with only four ladies and three gentlemen to attend me, in a battered old barge, as though they were shipping a hogshead of salted meat. I disliked it, but I understood the reason: Mary could not risk having any of my supporters take notice of me. She needed the assurance of the cheers for herself. I also understood that my supporters would have been reluctant to show their enthusiasm for me, afraid of endangering themselves as well as me. What a dismal state of affairs!

Soon after our arrival at Greenwich, I watched from the window of my apartments as leather-bound trunks and wooden chests were carried aboard another of the royal barges that would take Philip to Gravesend, where a Spanish ship lay at anchor. Suddenly one of my maids, a silly young girl named Alice, rushed into my chamber. "The king is here!" she gasped, forgetting to curtsy.

"King Philip? To see me?"

"Yes, madam."

Since visitors to my apartments were so rare, I was wearing a simple kirtle, scarcely dressed to receive anyone, much less the king. But I decided not to take time to change into a gown, for I felt this visit must be both brief and clandestine, lest the queen learn of his whereabouts.

"Tell His Majesty that I am pleased to receive him," I instructed the girl.

Of late, my glimpses of Philip had revealed to me a man suffering from dyspepsia. He often seemed dispirited and languorous, possibly from the strain of his wife's long and fruitless pregnancy. But this day he strode in full of vigor, his color high, his gait exuding vitality. He clasped my hand in his and bowed deeply.

"My lady Elizabeth," he said. At least that's what I thought he said, for although he had lived in England for over a year, he had mastered none of our language. Mary had attempted to teach him a few polite phrases, but he generally rendered them incomprehensible.

I replied in Latin, wishing him Godspeed in his journey. He thanked me, and then he said, "Her Majesty, the queen, has promised me that she will treat you with the honor and respect due you. I trust that your life will become more enjoyable."

Philip still grasped my hand and kept a slight pressure on it, so that I could not easily pull away. Little Alice was observing this scene with eyes as round as saucers, and instinct told me that although she did not understand the Latin words, every gesture and every change of tone of voice would be reported to someone, who would then report all of it to the queen. I snatched away my hand.

"And I will do all that I can to please my sister and to make your absence from her less intolerable," I said, employing the engaging smile that seemed to work so well with Philip.

"Then, farewell, dear madam," he said, and bowing once more, he left me.

Again at the window I watched as fifty fine English horses were led aboard the barge. Philip busied himself on deck, directing the final preparations. Hours later, as the barge cast off from the wharf, Philip waved his hat in the direction of the palace.

FOR WEEKS after Philip's departure, the queen behaved as though a death had occurred. Her entire court seemed to be in mourning. Nothing in my life changed.

I did everything I could to find my way into the queen's good graces. The week before my twenty-second birthday, I began a three-day fast in order to earn a pardon for my sins. The three days of swallowing only water were meant to impress Lady Susan Clarencieux and Lady Jane Dormer, whose scorn for me equaled the queen's.

Mary now pretended to be well disposed toward me, but I did not trust her, believing that her dislike of me had even deepened. Still, she did me one kindness—she restored to me three ladies-in-waiting who had been taken away when I was first sent to the Tower. Lady Marian, Lady Cynthia, and Lady Letitia wept joyously as I kissed each one. I thought them brave to return to my service, for any shadow of suspicion that was cast upon me would surely fall upon them as well. I heartily wished that the queen's kindness would have also restored to me Kat Ashley, from whom I had had no word since our parting many months earlier.

As autumn progressed the crops rotted in the fields, the harvest was the worst in many seasons, and still the rains fell. Floods carried off villagers as well as farm animals. Stores of grain and other provisions were spoiled. People began to go hungry.

Worse, Philip showed no sign of returning soon. Instead, he wrote from Flanders demanding that Mary make him king of England. She must have known how her privy council and her subjects would react if she gave in to Philip's demands: They would be furious. As much as she may have wished to please her husband, as deeply as she must have yearned for his return, Queen Mary refused.

Poor Mary! As much as I hated her, I can say that now and mean it sincerely. There were so many plots, so many conspirators who wished for her death, that she could trust no one, not even those closest to her. And nearly everyone had heard the latest rumors: King Philip was immensely enjoying life in the Netherlands and was often seen in the company of a certain Madame d'Aler. Philip seemed in no hurry to return to England and his adoring but stubborn wife.

MY LIFE SEEMED to hang suspended. I was no longer a prisoner, but I could not leave the palace without the queen's permission. The queen did not invite me to sup privately with her, although I was welcome to dine in the Great Hall of Greenwich Palace. When I did so scarcely anyone spoke to me. No one called upon me. Had it not been for my three ladies and a few empty-headed maids and serving girls, I would have been entirely alone.

I knew the reason: Everyone was afraid to be seen in my presence.

Only Sir William Cecil had the courage to call upon me. Sir William, no longer a privy councillor, now served in Parliament, where his reputation for honesty remained untarnished. One afternoon, as we walked in the palace gardens, he murmured, "Be careful, my lady Elizabeth."

"I am always careful, Sir William."

"And never more so than now."

I followed his advice. If I could avoid implication in the plots that swarmed like hornets around us at every hour of the day, I might yet survive to be queen. With his unspoken encouragement, I dared to hope once more.

CHAPTER 16

Hatfield

One afternoon Mary's favorite lady-in-waiting, Jane Dormer, appeared at my apartments. She brought me a letter from Queen Mary and waited impatiently while I read it. It was the word I had longed for, and had finally dared ask for, permission to return to Hatfield.

"So, my lady Elizabeth," Jane said scornfully, "you have gotten what you want, if not what you deserve."

I thanked her, ignoring her ill humor, and began at once to prepare to leave.

Two days later, as Lady Marian and Lady Letitia were overseeing the packing of my gowns and furs, a messenger arrived, summoning me to the queen's presence chamber. Any such summons always made me imagine the worst.

"Do you suppose she has changed her mind after all?" I asked Lady Marian anxiously.

"I think not," Marian reassured me. "Queen Mary intends to depart soon for London to open Parliament. I doubt that she wants you to accompany her."

Nevertheless, my knees shook as I knelt before the queen.

I was startled anew by my sister's appearance; she was pinched and thin, and her eyesight seemed to have grown worse. "Dear sister Elizabeth," she said, peering at me intently, "take with you not only our good wishes but these tokens of our affection."

Before the disapproving eyes of Susan Clarencieux and Jane Dormer, the queen placed a ruby ring upon my finger and presented me with a set of golden apostle spoons. *What a strange woman you are,* I thought, even as I thanked her heartily for the gifts. I never knew when she sent for me if I was to be punished or rewarded, thrown into prison or lavished with gifts.

Mary called old Father Francis to say a blessing over both of us, and when he'd finished, my sister rose and embraced me, formally and without warmth. I was free to go.

But I was still not free of anxiety.

All along the road from Greenwich to Hatfield, bells pealed and hundreds of supporters turned out to cheer for me. Traveling in my company was my former tutor,

Roger Ascham. As the joyous welcome grew more boisterous, Ascham pulled up his horse beside mine and
said, "If the queen hears of this, she will not be pleased."

The cheers gladdened my heart but also caused me
some misgivings. I acknowledged Ascham's warning
and called to several of my gentlemen. "Go among the
people," I instructed them, "and try to restrain their
celebration."

But the crowds would not be quieted. Their enthusiasm was music to my ears all the way to Hatfield. It
was at that moment that the fragile flicker of hope I had
been nurturing for months now burst into flame: *I will
triumph and I will rule.*

NEARLY TWO YEARS had passed since I'd first left Hatfield for London. During my first days back in the
palace, I walked happily from chamber to chamber, assuring myself that everything was well ordered, the
kitchens provisioned, the outbuildings in good repair,
the animals cared for.

Best of all, Kat Ashley was allowed to return. She
arrived dusty and disheveled from her journey, and I
rushed straight into her arms. For the next few days I
could not bear to have her leave my sight. Also back in
my service were Thomas Parry and his sister Blanche. I
hired an Italian tutor, Battista Castiglione, to improve
my fluency in that language. Roger Ascham gratified my
need for intellectual discourse, as we read together. Once
again Lady Marian and Lady Letitia and I rode out upon

the heath. I loved to give my favorite gelding full rein to jump brooks and hedgerows. Letitia always kept up, but Marian was left far behind and grumbling. Surrounded as I was now by my old friends, it was almost as though the events of the past two years had not occurred.

Nevertheless, I remained mindful of Sir William Cecil's warning. For every friend in my household, there was a spy for the queen.

I made up my mind to give these spies nothing to report. I heard Mass daily and made my confession weekly, as I had when I was living under the queen's nose. I had no intention of becoming a martyr, and so I continued to live outwardly as a Catholic. This deception was not difficult for me, because God knew what was truly in my heart.

I WAS NOT invited to court at Christmas, nor did I wish to be. I'd had quite enough of the queen's prying eyes. Instead, I amused myself at Hatfield. Musicians entertained us on every one of the twelve nights of Yuletide, and a troupe of traveling players performed a masque to welcome the new year.

In the early months of 1556, I was told, Queen Mary remained in seclusion with a few of her women. The only occasions for leaving her private chambers were to attend Mass *nine times a day* in the chapel royal. She was now forty years old.

Famine spread, as did the unrest. Mary believed this was a sign from God that she must do even more to rid the kingdom of heresy, and so the burnings continued. I prayed that someone would stop her, but no one dared. Hundreds of suspected heretics crowded the prisons, many of them condemned to die at the stake. Unlike a hanging or a beheading, which always drew noisy crowds, the long and agonizing burning deaths attracted few witnesses. Instead of turning people back to Catholicism, as Mary intended, the suffering of these martyrs seemed to deepen the faith of those who shared their Protestant beliefs. Word went out that any who sympathized with the sufferings of the condemned were to be arrested and burned as well.

"When I am queen, I swear before God, nothing like this will happen," I promised Kat. Although such thoughts were often in my mind, it was the first time I had uttered these words aloud: *when I am queen.*

WHENEVER THERE WAS talk of another plot against Mary, I became apprehensive. I heard that my name was always mentioned prominently, even though I had no part in these things. I was determined to stay as far from the plots and intrigue as possible. If I would live to be queen, I could not afford to take that risk! The fate of Thomas Wyatt had taught me that.

But no matter how much I wished to do so, I could not control Mary's enemies. I'd been back at Hatfield scarcely six months when I again came under suspicion. Yet another member of the Dudley family—Sir Henry, Robin's brother—had gone to France to raise an invasion force against Queen Mary. Once more Edward Courtenay was implicated in the plot. *Does that fool never learn?* I marveled.

This latest plot seemed to involve many of my acquaintances and even a number of my servants. I wasn't surprised when I learned that the privy council had ordered a search of Somerset House, my London mansion. As uneasy as I felt, I was certain nothing would be found to incriminate me.

Then, a week after the search, two dozen of the queen's guardsmen thundered up to the gates of Hatfield Palace. As I rushed to the entryway, they called loudly for Mistress Catherine Ashley.

"For what reason?" I demanded.

"Charges of sedition, madam!" shouted the captain of the guard.

Kat, inciting rebellion? "On what evidence?" I shouted in response.

Hearing the raised voices, Kat appeared at my side, her face gray with fright. The captain glanced at Kat and then back to me. "A cabinet filled with printed material insulting and dishonoring Her Majesty, the queen, and the Holy Catholic Church. It is said to belong to that woman," he said, pointing rudely at Kat, who uttered a shrill cry and collapsed at my feet.

The guardsman paid her no attention. He unrolled a parchment and read from it. "Also ordered to be taken, one Battista Castiglione, listed here as professor of Italian, and one Francis Verney, steward."

"And the charges against them?" I asked, struggling for control.

"Sedition, madam."

I was stunned. *How many times,* I thought as the weeping prisoners were dragged away, *must I watch as my most trusted servants are subjected to abuse, insult, and imprisonment?*

My helplessness angered me and reduced me to tears. But I could do nothing but await the consequence of this latest outrage.

My friends denied all the accusations, and naturally they were not believed. Kat swore that she knew nothing of the anti-Catholic pamphlets, broadsides, and mocking ballads discovered in the cabinet. But once again she found herself a prisoner on my account, held this time in Fleet Prison. Castiglione was eventually released—he confessed only that he had traveled to London on my behalf to purchase lute strings. But poor Verney was tried and sentenced to death. (He was later pardoned, but at the time neither he nor I knew if he would survive this ordeal.)

Then, unbelievably, Queen Mary sent her emissaries to me with the gift of a diamond ring and an apology for any disruption that might have been caused me by the arrest of my people! *Disruption!* I wanted so badly to fling both ring and apology in their faces, but of course I did neither.

Next the emissaries bid me come to court, at Mary's invitation. I knew it wasn't Mary's desire to see her dear sister that had prompted this invitation. Mary wanted more than anything to lock me in the Tower and have me questioned until I broke. But she was too shrewd to risk angering my supporters, who, she knew, grew daily in numbers and were now in the thousands—without my having raised a finger or said a word. I guessed her plan: She would wait for me to set my own trap and fall into it. She would have to wait a long time. I knew better than to take that bait.

Immediately I wrote a note to the queen, thanking her for the gift of the ring and for her kind invitation, and begging to be excused, due to ill health. "I suffer from a catarrh," I explained, and dismissed the emissaries with the letter.

Mary may have believed my thin excuse, or she may not have. In any case she next wrote to me that, as an unmarried woman, I needed the protection of a governor. I understood this to mean another jailer, and I half expected Sir Henry Bedingfield to appear at the gates of Hatfield. Instead, the queen appointed a wealthy and sober gentleman named Sir Thomas Pope to this duty.

Although I awaited his arrival with some uneasiness, Sir Thomas turned out to be well educated, worldly, and generous. I found him a sympathetic companion who went out of his way to arrange for all sorts of masques and recitals of music for my entertainment.

Thus occupied at Hatfield, I was far from the intrigues of London when ten men accused in the most recent conspiracy were executed and their heads mounted on pikes along London Bridge. Edward Courtenay, who

seemed to show up in every plot but unaccountably re-
tained the queen's sympathy, was allowed to leave the
country. In September he became ill and died in Italy;
poison was suspected. Although I had not wished for his
death, my mind was put at ease knowing that I would
never again be associated with one of Courtenay's ill-
conceived plots.

For four tension-filled months, I prayed daily that I
would be left alone by the queen. Then abruptly Sir
Thomas Pope was dismissed from my household. At
the same time Kat was released from Fleet Prison. None
of the charges against her could be proved, and I eagerly
awaited her return to Hatfield. Once she was safely
back, I resumed my studies of Italian with Castiglione,
continued my needlework with Kat, played upon my
lute with Lady Marian, rode my gelding out upon the
heath with Lady Cynthia, went hawking with Lady
Letitia, and discussed the classics with Roger Ascham.

And once again I dared dream of the day that I would
be queen.

In november Queen Mary summoned me to Whitehall Palace. This was not an invitation that could be politely declined; it was an order that had to be obeyed.
With much agitation I set out along the dusty road for
London, accompanied by two hundred horsemen out-
fitted in the new livery I had devised: crimson satin
trimmed with black velvet.

The summer past had been so hot and dry that the

tender young plants withered and perished in the crusted earth. A year earlier endless rains had destroyed the harvest, but this year there would be no harvest at all. "Two bad years in a row," observed the knight who rode beside me. "Famine will surely take its toll."

But I was too distracted by worries about my coming interview with the queen to realize then just how serious the problem was.

When I'd left Queen Mary's court to go home to Hatfield, my sister appeared ill and tired. Now she looked even worse: Her face was haggard, her brow knit in a permanent frown. After the rituals of bowing and kneeling had been accomplished, the queen motioned for me to come near. She took my face between her two hands and held it while she stared at me. I had no idea if she intended to kiss me or spit at me. Her breath was foul, and I had to force myself not to draw back.

"Comely thing, are you not?" she growled in her deep voice.

"If it please Your Majesty to say so," I replied.

She released me and pushed me away. I sank to my knees and waited, the blood pounding in my ears. "It is said that men admire your beauty, Elizabeth. Although," she added, "we think that beauty is too strong a word. Your nose is too long and too thin to be called beautiful."

"Yes, Your Majesty."

"But comely enough, we should think, to attract a husband. And that is what we shall do, dear sister. Get you a husband."

So that's what this was about! She had brought me from Hatfield to tell me that she planned to force me to marry!

"Has Your Majesty a candidate in mind who would not object to a wife with a long, thin nose?" I asked.

"And a sharp tongue," she added. "It is your tongue that most men would object to."

"Yes, Your Majesty."

For a time the queen was silent. Mary had developed a troubling habit of staring. I didn't know if she had fallen into a reverie or forgotten I was there. I remained on my knees and waited.

"We wish devoutly that you accept the suit of Emmanuel Philibert, duke of Savoy, to be your husband. King Philip is in agreement with our wishes."

This was the same duke who had come to England to "pluck the fruit" two years earlier, while I was a prisoner at Woodstock. Apparently he had not given up. "I am pleased that the duke thinks well of me," I said carefully, my thoughts racing. I calculated each reply I might make, weighing the possible consequences.

Mary hesitated and pulled at her lower lip. This was another irritating habit. "Savoy has much to recommend him," she said. "He is the most highly regarded of the Emperor Charles's generals."

"With all due respect, Your Majesty," I began, "I cannot marry the duke."

"And why not? He would make you an admirable husband, Elizabeth. You would do well to choose him."

I paused a moment to summon my courage. Then I plunged ahead. "I have made up my mind not to marry," I stated in a clear, firm voice. "It is not a choice of this man or that one but of no husband at all."

Mary smiled sourly. "Perhaps you wish to take a vow of celibacy, then?" she said. "Withdraw to a nunnery?"

"No, madam," I said. "I simply wish not to marry."

"You refuse the order of your queen?" she snarled, her bitterness breaking through. "You refuse the order of your sovereign, who holds over you the power of life and death? Perhaps you would change your mind after a few months in the Tower."

The Tower! The queen guessed my deepest fear and played upon it. But I resisted her tactic. Deciding that tears were now called for, I began to weep. "I remain obedient in all things to Your Majesty," I cried, reaching for her sympathy. "But, I beg you, do not force me to marry!"

Mary gave me another of her long, hard stares. Then abruptly she waved me away. "Go back to Hatfield," she snapped. "This interview has been of no use."

The next day I returned to the country, having negotiated once more a difficult stretch of road but never sure that the queen might not change her mind, as she had before.

I also vowed that Queen Mary had seen the last of my tears, real or feigned. I would not weep in her presence again.

CHAPTER 17

King Philip's Return

Christmas of 1556 found me once again at court, invited, no doubt, because Philip had sent instructions to the queen to do so. I took with me a number of new gowns and petticoats, made to my order in France. I felt that it was now time to show whatever friends I had at court a new Elizabeth, strong and able, no longer in the shadows. Therefore I chose the loveliest shades of blue and green, russet and yellow, to set off the elegant jewels my father had left me.

My finery was wasted on this court. Never have I witnessed such lackluster Yuletide observances—I cannot use the word *festivities*—as Mary moved woodenly through the rites and customs. She seemed barely able to mutter "wassail" when the traditional toasts were drunk.

Fortunately for me, among the guests was Anne of Cleves, with whom I passed a number of pleasant hours. Her gowns were somewhat out-of-date, as they had always been, but her jewels were magnificent. As usual, she was an astute observer of court life. We sat near a fire in the drafty chamber that had been assigned to Anne, our hands busy with needlework and our tongues seeking those subjects that interested us both.

"Hers is not an easy lot," Anne murmured, indicating the queen, "being married to such a man."

I smiled; if anyone would recognize the difficulties of marriage to an impossible husband, it was my father's fourth wife.

"King Philip has been gone for a year and a half," Anne observed. "He puts off the queen with promises and excuses. The gossips tell me that he has been behaving rather badly with the ladies of Flanders."

"Does the queen know of this?" I asked.

"She does," Anne replied.

"Perhaps she even expects it. But she fears that one of his flirtations will turn to love. Indeed, she fears that it already has."

"And has it?"

"Christina of Denmark, duchess of Lorraine, is said to be quite beautiful."

"Is Philip in love with the duchess?" I whispered.

"So I am told."

For a while we plied our stitches in companionable silence, and I pondered this bit of gossip.

"Nonetheless," Anne continued, "King Philip will soon return to England. He has made up his mind to go to war against France. He needs English money to finance it."

"And the queen has agreed to provide it?"

Anne of Cleves raised her eyebrows. "He has made it a condition of his return. She wants him to come back."

"Badly, it would seem."

"Very badly." Anne sighed. "At all costs. And while he is here"—she glanced at me from the corner of her eye—"he means to see you married off. Probably to the duke of Savoy. You are aware of this?"

I nodded. "But I do not intend to marry," I said.

Anne of Cleves laid aside her needlework and looked at me directly. "It was once rumored that, had Mary died in childbirth, King Philip would have married you. You are important to him for political reasons. It is at his insistence that Mary has not found some reason to have you executed for treason. You owe Philip your life. But he will attempt to persuade you, by honeyed tones or by threats, to change your mind about marriage. Can you hold to your decision in the face of his will?"

"My power to refuse is greater than his power to insist," I said passionately.

"Then I wish you strength and courage, my dear Elizabeth."

Our conversation ended when our maids entered the chamber to remind us that the time had come to change into our gowns for the New Year's banquet. I would wear yellow silk embroidered with pearls, opening upon a petticoat of palest green.

The queen, although appearing low-spirited, was, as always, generous with her gifts. I received from her a golden goblet set with pearls, identical to the goblet she presented to Anne of Cleves.

SOON AFTER Twelfth Night I made my farewells and returned to Hatfield. There I remained until March, when I received the news that King Philip was returning to England. I was invited to the celebration, and I accepted. It was another opportunity to show myself to England's nobility as the queen's sister and next in line for the throne.

A royal barge waited for Philip when his ship landed at Dover and conveyed him to Greenwich. There a thirty-two gun salute greeted him, as did a large contingent of the queen's cheering courtiers. The queen herself appeared to be in a state of rapture at the sight of her husband.

The next day, as the royal procession approached London, church bells pealed and the guns in the Tower boomed. The queen had ordered the choirs of every church to sing Te Deums in thanksgiving for the king's return. We then proceeded to Richmond Palace. For once I was not shipped like a bale of wool on a leaking punt but on a newly painted barge decked with flowers. It was an occasion to dress splendidly, and I wore a gown of russet silk with a black velvet stomacher richly embroidered in gold. Crowds lined the banks of the Thames, cheering the royal procession.

On the day of the great festival in Philip's honor, I made a good show of enjoying myself, although my heart was far from easy. I warily awaited the moment the king might press me to agree to a betrothal.

When the festival was ended, Philip, Mary, and I rode in state to Whitehall Palace. I stayed in London for a few days, as required. During that time no word was said of a betrothal. Again I sought out Anne of Cleves, who seemed to have diverse sources of gossip. But she had no news for me, and I returned to Hatfield somewhat relieved.

ONE AFTERNOON a troupe of minstrels appeared at my gates. A young fellow carrying a gittern informed the guards that he had been sent to perform for me. He was turned away, but he continued to insist. I agreed to see him, but remembering the "priest" sent by Thomas Wyatt, I was on my guard.

"Who sent you?" I asked.

"A friend who offers this token," said the boy, presenting a velvet sack. In it was a golden goblet set with pearls, identical to the one Mary had given me at New Year's. It had been sent by Anne of Cleves.

"Come," I told the boy, "and sing me your song."

The others of his troupe made to follow, but I turned them back.

When we were alone, the minstrel strummed an awkward chord and stammered a few off-key lines. "This is painful to my ears!" I exclaimed. Suddenly the lad pulled off his cap to reveal long golden curls. It was Lady Cecily, lady-in-waiting to Anne of Cleves.

Much amused by her errand, Lady Cecily assured me that for her safety she had traveled with several knights, who were disguised as musicians in the troupe. "My errand is to bring to you messages that Madame Anne could send safely by no other means."

"Then tell me."

"Two visitors have arrived in London," she said as we sat in my bedchamber, eating sweetmeats. "One is Margaret, duchess of Parma, a cousin of King Philip. The other is Christina of Denmark, duchess of Lorraine."

"The king's mistress? Surely not!"

"Their arrival much surprised and angered the queen. She assigned them to chambers as far from the royal apartments as possible."

"But why have they come?"

"To take you back to the Continent, my lady," said Cecily, "to hand you over for wife to the duke of Savoy."

I was nearly speechless.

"You know of the duke?" Lady Cecily inquired.

"I have not had the pleasure of meeting him."

"He has scarcely a farthing to his name," Cecily said.

"And that is why he wants to marry you. He is in love with your wealth."

"I would rather spend the rest of my life in the Tower than submit," I said with some heat.

"You may not need to resort to anything so drastic," said the lady, nibbling a confit. "The queen has no wish for you to marry Savoy."

I was astonished. "She has not? Then she has changed her mind."

"So it would seem. Now that Queen Mary has failed to produce an heir, she knows that when she enters into a negotiation for your betrothal, she will have no choice but to declare you the legitimate and trueborn daughter of King Henry the Eighth."

"As indeed I am."

"Begging your pardon, my lady, but your sister does not acknowledge that. She still insists that Mark Smeaton was your natural father. And she holds your mother in"—here Cecily hesitated—"less than high regard. The queen holds that you are illegitimate, but as a bastard you have no value in a marriage negotiation. Even an impoverished duke might flinch from marrying a bastard, who cannot become queen and make him the king. The queen cannot bring herself to declare you legitimate," said Cecily, "but the king will try to influence her, in order to have you married."

I was silent for a moment. "If Mary declares me legitimate, she will then try to force me to marry against my will. If she does not declare me legitimate, I cannot inherit the throne."

"What shall you do, Lady Elizabeth?" Cecily asked.

"No matter what Mary does, I shall not marry," I said. *"And someday I shall become queen."*

WHEN I RETURNED to court at Easter, I could sense the unease all around me. The banquets and balls that Mary had arranged to commence at Easter and to continue through the Feast of Saint Mark were marred by bad feelings. Mary seemed sunk into melancholy. Philip chose this time to inform me that I would marry the duke of Savoy. So the king had convinced Mary after all! What would she not do for him?

"My lord," I declared firmly, "with all due respect to your wishes and the wishes of my sister, I cannot marry the duke."

"Cannot? Pray, why can you not, my lady?"

"Because I will not marry. Therefore I cannot marry Philibert or anyone else."

"I beg you to reconsider, Elizabeth. The duke holds you in highest regard. Your life will be pleasant, and you will find the Continent an agreeable place to live."

"No matter how agreeable the gentleman or his home, I will not marry the duke of Savoy," I said evenly. "Let us end this conversation."

Philip glared at me threateningly. "By God, woman, if you refuse to marry him, I will see that you are returned to the Tower!"

I knew that he might very well do that. But he might be trying to frighten me. I took a deep breath and defied him: "Imprison me then, sir. I have endured prison before. It can be no worse than marriage." Then I bowed and dared to walk away, leaving him open-mouthed and staring.

I had to find out what was happening. Anne of Cleves was ill and had not come to court. Desperate for news, I sent a message to Sir William Cecil, begging him to meet me in secret. Several anxious days passed until I received a reply. Lady Letitia dressed me in a servant's rough brown kirtle and threw a shawl over my hair. Sir William waited in the scullery, rather poorly disguised as an egg peddler.

"Tell me what is happening!" I pleaded.

"The queen is ecstatic to have her husband back with her," Sir William said, adding dryly, "but I understand that the privy council is somewhat less delighted. And not at all eager to enter a war against France. Philip and the queen have labored for weeks to persuade the privy council to support him. Eventually they will give in."

"And on the matter of the duke of Savoy?"

Cecil stroked his beard, too well barbered for any peddler. "Philip ordered the queen to compel you to marry the duke. She refused his order. He then accused her of failing in her marital duty to obey him. The council will not force you to marry a man who is half Spanish and half French by blood. Neither half is loved by the English. For now, at least, you are safe."

"Thank you, my friend," I said, weak with relief. "Now, tell me—what is the price of your eggs?"

"Of that I have not any idea, madam," he said, bowing. He strode away, leaving the basket at my feet.

I WAS WAITING to be dismissed from court when the queen summoned me to her chambers.

"You wish to return to Hatfield, dear sister?" she asked.

"When Your Majesty permits," I replied, uneasy, as I always felt with her, although her tone was kind.

"We have not visited Hatfield in years," said Queen Mary somewhat wistfully. "Is it still such a lovely place?"

"The loveliest on earth," I replied. Then I added impulsively, "Your Majesty would do me a great honor to come to Hatfield to see for herself." It did not occur to me that she would accept my invitation.

But Mary smiled. "And so we shall. Expect our arrival within the fortnight."

"With pleasure, madam," I lied.

God help me! My enemy was coming to visit.

FOR DAYS MY household worked ceaselessly to prepare for the queen's arrival and to devise ways to entertain her. It was a time of little sleep and much worry.

The boys of Saint Paul's School would perform a play in Latin. I would present a recital on the virginals that once belonged to my father. Several banquets would be served, although I doubted that I could procure Mary's favorite, wild boar meat, in time.

Everything was in readiness on a brilliant spring day when the royal entourage wound its way to the palace gates with trumpets blaring and pennants snapping in the strong breeze. I went out to welcome the queen, still wondering, *Why does she want to come here?*

It turned out that what Mary really wanted was to play cards. The queen was especially fond of primero, and she gambled recklessly on each hand. Over the next several days, we each lost and won back a small fortune.

We talked of little of consequence. I discovered quickly that Mary loved to hear me speak of King Philip. Her spirits lifted at any mention of him. She laced her conversation with constant references to "our husband, the king." But there was no mention of the duke of Savoy, the duchess of Lorraine, the coming war against France, or of Mary's own poor health.

At the end of five days, the queen gathered up her retinue and departed. It was, I thought, a successful visit. During the hours we spent together, I nearly forgot that the queen hated me and that I thought no more kindly of her.

CHAPTER 18

The Death of the Queen

Soon after the queen returned to London, I heard that the duchesses were gone. According to one report the queen had ordered Christina of Denmark to pack her bags and leave. According to another the duchesses, forbidden to drag me off as Savoy's bride, had gotten bored and sailed away.

There was more news: England had declared war against France. Sir William Cecil told me about it when he came to Hatfield early in June.

"So the privy council has approved Philip's plan?" I asked.

"The queen was relentless. She took each councillor aside separately from the others and threatened death if he did not agree to the plan. She reminded me of her father in her method," he said with a faint smile.

"Apparently her method succeeded."

"It did, but I do not think that the war will succeed. King Philip leaves within the month. Then we shall see."

I heard from Lady Marian the story of King Philip's departure. When she returned from Greenwich, she agreed to ride out with me. On this occasion I handled my mount sedately, for I was more interested in Marian's tales of court than I was in an exciting ride.

"In the last weeks Queen Mary and King Philip were constantly in each other's company," she told me. "They took their meals together, they attended Mass together several times a day, and they worked tirelessly in preparation for the coming battles with the French.

"The queen could not bear to be out of his sight," Marian continued. "She adores him beyond all reason! Early in July the queen accompanied her husband to Dover. She slept by his side each night of the journey. Some say that she still hopes for a child. When Philip sailed with the tide at three o'clock on the morning of the sixth of July, Mary clung to him until the last possible moment. She made no effort to hide her tears."

"And the king?" I asked. "Was he distraught as well?"

"He treated the queen with great tenderness," said Marian. "But it was clear he could scarcely wait to be gone."

———

FOR A TIME the news from the war was encouraging, but our jubilation was short-lived. With the chill rains of November came the first cases of an illness marked by catarrh and feverish delirium. The illness spread quickly and was to claim thousands of lives before it had run its course. The rising number of deaths caused my Protestant neighbors to remark that this was surely a curse sent by God to punish the queen for her sins.

Among those whose lives were taken that winter was my old friend, Anne of Cleves. Lady Cecily, dressed in mourning, brought me the news.

"Before her death she asked me to deliver to you these remembrances," Lady Cecily said. A servant set a finely wrought wooden case upon a table, and Cecily herself opened it. Laid against a background of black velvet was a splendid collection of jewels—ropes of pearls, brooches set with diamonds and emeralds, rings of gold set with rubies, headpieces decked with sapphires. I owned many jewels, but these were truly magnificent.

"The dowager queen cared deeply for you, my lady Elizabeth," Cecily told me.

I made Cecily a gift of a gold bracelet from Anne's collection. "Strength and courage," I said, clasping it upon her wrist, and after many tears, she rode away. Days later I learned that, on her way to London, Lady Cecily, too, was stricken. She died within a fortnight.

ALTHOUGH I DID NOT myself fall victim to the fever that raged all around us, I decided not to risk a journey to Greenwich for Yuletide and instead observed the season quietly with my own household.

Sir William Cecil arrived a few days after Twelfth Night in the midst of a howling blizzard. Although I was pleased, as always, to see him, I could not imagine that he would have ventured out in such foul weather without a serious purpose. His eyes were sad, and his shoulders slumped as though under a heavy weight.

When everything possible had been done to warm and cheer him, I dismissed the servants. "What has happened?" I asked.

"Calais," he said bitterly. "It has fallen to the French."

"Calais!" I cried. "It cannot be!"

Calais had belonged to England for more than two hundred years. It was the point on the Continent that lay closest to England. This fortified city was also the center of the English wool trade and therefore of great economic importance. It was thought to be invincible. And now we had lost it!

Then, having delivered this first shocking piece of news, Cecil had another: "Her Majesty, the queen, has announced that she is with child."

"Queen Mary is pregnant?" I asked incredulously. "But surely—"

"Surely she believes that she is," Cecil said wearily. "She told the privy council that she has suspected her condition for some time, but she waited until she was absolutely certain."

"When is the child expected?" I asked, utterly shaken.

"In March."

I DID NOT believe that my sister was pregnant, and I think few others believed it either. Naturally no one could discuss this openly. For the last pregnancy I had spent the months before the anticipated birth embroidering a wardrobe of tiny garments for the infant. This time I decided to stitch a christening gown, although I had no faith whatsoever that it would ever be worn by a child of Mary's.

At the end of February, as custom decreed, I made my way to Greenwich Palace in a large company of my gentlemen and ladies-in-waiting. I dreaded this lying-in, if that's what it was. The queen received me formally, with neither outward malice nor affection. I saw that her belly was indeed swollen, yet I doubted that she carried a child. She looked very ill. Once again the long wait began.

I foresaw no good end to it. There would be the fruitless wait. There would be no child. I could scarcely imagine what my sister's state of mind would be when she was forced to acknowledge her delusion. Would the madness of the burnings intensify even further?

But what if I was wrong? If my sister did give birth to a living child, my future was ruined.

Numb with worry, I waited. The entire court did.

Philip did not return. Instead, he sent the count of

Feria to attend to his wife's needs. Whatever else the count accomplished, he caused Queen Mary's favorite lady-in-waiting, Jane Dormer, to fall in love with him. Jane was a handsome woman of wealth and position but as yet unmarried. Mary would not allow her favorite to wed, always claiming that none of Jane's suitors was good enough. With Philip far away, Jane often slept in the royal bedchamber with Mary.

This time Mary did not interfere. That romance was the one happy outcome of the whole cheerless affair.

By Easter the queen had once again to admit that she was not with child. Her condition was diagnosed as dropsy, her belly swollen with fluid. She must have realized that she was dying, and she sank into deep despondency. I returned quietly to Hatfield to await the next development and to fend off the marriage proposals with which I was still being tormented. The latest was from the king of Sweden, who sent an envoy to offer the king's son Eric, duke of Finland. I refused it as I had refused all others.

Yet even as I waited, I knew that as long as my sister remained alive, it was within her power to prevent my becoming queen. The Tower still loomed as a threatening possibility.

IN SEPTEMBER I observed my twenty-fifth birthday. As the months passed, Mary's condition worsened. Unless I made a serious mistake to trigger her anger or Mary succumbed to total madness, I now believed that I would soon become queen. I thought of little else.

I spent many hours considering who would assist me in the enormous task that lay ahead. Yet, even as death approached, my sister refused to name me as her successor. I was still her enemy, as I had been for twenty-five years.

The queen yielded, touchingly, on one issue: She finally granted her dear Jane Dormer permission to marry her sweetheart, the count of Feria. Mary's only regret, she said, was that she would not live to see the wedding.

And, as though to hold death at bay, Queen Mary continued her struggle to rid the kingdom of heretics. The last five would burn at the stake early in November.

THE ROAD TO Hatfield was clogged with visitors. I received them, I listened, but I said little. I did not wish to reveal the anxiety I felt, lest it be seen as weakness. The goal that had seemed so far away was now within reach. I was ready. And yet, whenever I allowed myself to consider the huge weight about to fall upon my shoulders, I felt cold with apprehension. I spent many hours in prayer, as fervent as those I had uttered when I was in fear for my life.

For the five years since Queen Mary's coronation, when I knew that by rights I was next in line for the throne, I had thought daily—hourly!—of what it would mean to be queen. For the five years of her reign, all my efforts had been to survive her jealousy and hatred of me. Now, as the queen's life slowly ebbed away, I became less afraid for my own life. Now my greatest fear was for England.

It was in the course of long conversations with Sir William Cecil that I began to grasp fully the problems facing the kingdom—and me, her future queen. The aftermath of the burnings, the Catholics who dreaded a Protestant on the throne. The depleted treasury, the money squandered on the war with France, the loss of Calais. The years of poor harvests, and the resulting famine and poverty that had reached every corner of the kingdom. The councillors who thought a woman unfit to rule—even Cecil had no faith in my ability to govern.

"You must marry as soon as possible, madam," he said.

"Hear me well, Sir William," I told him, "for I shall not say this to you again: *I shall not marry.*"

Sir Cecil merely bowed and made no reply.

Among those who called upon me was Robin Dudley. The years had, if anything, improved his dark good looks. I received him in the privy garden. We exchanged pleasantries, and I asked after the health of his wife, Amy Dudley.

"She is well, madam." Then he took my hand and kissed it. "I swear my loyalty to you, my lady Elizabeth," he said. "I have much to say to you. Come, let us walk together."

We left the privy garden by way of the lime walk, strolling past the knot garden and away from the palace. The trees were bright with autumn foliage, the late roses still in bloom. At length we reached the ancient oak some distance from the palace where I often came to read and to think. I seated myself upon a stone bench and waited to hear what Robin had to say.

"Madam, although you have no rivals, you have many enemies. Until now you have spent your life enduring the enmity of your sister. That battle will soon end. But in truth you have only begun the fight." Robin stepped closer, so that he was gazing directly into my eyes. "If you wish to survive, you must force your advisers to obey you. The common people need no persuasion—you are the daughter of their beloved King Henry the Eighth. But you must show the nobility that you are able to rule them."

Suddenly Robin Dudley dropped to his knees, his cap in his hands. "I pledge myself to fight for your throne, madam," he said. "I am your servant unto death."

"I much prefer your loyalty in life, Robin," I said. "Can you promise me that?"

"With all my heart."

Our eyes remain locked. "And you, Robin," I asked him, curious to hear his reply, "think you I must marry in order to rule?"

"No, Elizabeth," he said quietly. "You are everything that England needs."

———

AT LAST CAME the visitor I had been waiting for. Jane Dormer arrived with a large retinue dressed in the queen's livery. Now that Jane was in love, some of the hardness around her mouth had softened, but still she made no attempt to conceal her dislike for me.

"Her Majesty, Queen Mary, has sent me to you with this token," she said, presenting me with a heavy gold ring.

I held the ring in the palm of my hand, feeling its weight. "And what does this ring signify?" I asked.

"The queen has named you her successor." Jane halted to collect herself.

So she has done it after all! I exulted silently.

"The queen begs that you maintain the old religion, take care of her servants, and pay her debts," Jane continued when she was able, "and she desires your promise that you will do these things."

Maintain the old religion? Surely Mary knew better, and just as surely Jane did, too. Nevertheless, I knelt beside Jane. "I do solemnly promise that I will carry out the queen's wishes in all things," I said. With this one last lie to my sister, I slipped Mary's gold ring on my thumb.

TODAY THERE IS a damp chill in the air. I was seated again by the ancient oak where Robin Dudley had pledged me his loyalty when I saw a group of men making their way toward me. Among them were Sir William Paget and the earl of Arundel, dressed in mourning. I rose to greet them.

"The queen is dead," said the men in voices rough with feeling. "Long live the queen!"

The moment had arrived. My sister was dead, no longer my enemy. I had survived this first great challenge. Yet, as long as I had prepared for this moment, expected it, feared it, and desired it, I was overwhelmed with emotion. I fell to my knees and recited in Latin the first words that came to my mind, the words of the psalmist: *This is the Lord's doing; it is marvelous in our eyes!*

Today I am Elizabeth, queen of England.

HISTORICAL NOTE

QUEEN MARY was buried on the fourteenth of December, 1558, in Westminster Abbey with the full rites of the Roman Catholic Church. On the fifteenth of January, a date selected by her astrologer, Dr. Dee, Mary's hated sister, Elizabeth, was crowned queen, beginning a reign that would last for forty-five years. It became one of the most remarkable periods in English history.

During Elizabeth's reign England flourished. The Protestant Church of England was firmly reestablished, English ships decisively defeated the Spanish Armada, Francis Drake and Walter Raleigh explored and colonized the New World, and William Shakespeare created some of the most brilliant works of literature in the English language.

Vain and ruthless, headstrong and witty, beautiful and hot tempered, Queen Elizabeth never married. There were rumors of love affairs, one with Robin Dudley, who served Elizabeth as master of the horse. Robin's wife, Amy, died under questionable circumstances, and once again Elizabeth found herself under a cloud of suspicion. When Elizabeth did not marry Robin Dudley, he began a romance with Lettice Knollys, the beautiful young daughter of Elizabeth's cousin Catherine.

Queen Elizabeth died on the twenty-third of March, 1603, at the age of sixty-nine. Like her sister, Queen Elizabeth delayed naming her successor until the last moment. She left the crown to James, son of Mary, Queen of Scots, Elizabeth's cousin. Mary had been the one serious threat to Elizabeth's throne, and Elizabeth had reluctantly put her cousin to death in 1587.

Elizabeth I is buried beside her sister, Mary, in a tomb built for them by the new king, James I, in the Henry VII Chapel in Westminster Abbey. The two sisters and queens share this epitaph:

> *Consorts both in throne and grave,*
> *here rest we two sisters,*
> *Elizabeth and Mary,*
> *in the hope of one resurrection.*

Mary, Bloody Mary

A wrenching riches-to-rags story

Mary Tudor is a beautiful young princess in a grand palace filled with servants. She is accustomed to sparkling jewels, beautiful gowns, and lavish parties. Then, suddenly, she is banished by her father, King Henry VIII, to live in a cold, lonely place without money, new clothes, or even her mother.

At first it seems like a terrible mistake. Even when her father has a public and humiliating affair with a bewitching woman, Mary remains hopeful. But when he abandons her mother, then marries his mistress and has a child with her, Mary begins to lose faith. And now, dressed in rags, she is summoned back to the palace to be a serving maid to her new baby stepsister.

Told in the voice of the young Mary, Carolyn Meyer's first book in the Young Royals series is a compassionate historical novel about love and loss, jealousy and fear— and a girl's struggle with forces far beyond her control.

ABA's Pick of the Lists
An ALA Best Book for Young Adults
A *Kirkus Reviews* Children's Book of Special Note
An NCSS-CBC Notable Children's Trade Book in the
    Field of Social Studies
A New York Public Library Book for the Teen Age

Turn the page to see Mary's dramatic change of fate....

THIS WAS MY FIRST TIME in the palace in nearly five years. It was a shock to realize how far I had fallen! Five years earlier I had still been Princess of Wales, still accorded all the honor and privilege of my rank. Now I was nothing, nobody, no better than a servant myself. I had not been invited because I was wanted but because tradition required it. And it was an opportunity for Queen Anne to show her power over me.

When we arrived my ladies and I were given poorly furnished chambers in a remote part of the palace that I had never seen before. I was hungry but had no chance to send for some bread and ale because I was summoned to the queen's chambers.

"I shall call upon Lady Anne when I've had a chance to refresh myself," I told the messenger.

"Her Majesty the queen commands you to pay your respects at once," the servant insisted.

I followed the servant to the queen's chamber of presence.

Since the beginning of her eighth month of pregnancy, Anne had been required to stay in these chambers with a few waiting women whose unhappy duty it was to keep her entertained. Tapestries and hangings covered every window and even the ceiling; the chamber was oppressively dark and stifling. Anne reclined awkwardly on a couch piled with silk pillows. Behind her a pair of wide oak doors opened to an inner chamber, similarly draped and darkened. In the midst of that second room stood a magnificent bed. I recognized it at once—it was my mother's bed, given her by my father at the time of my birth. Now it would become the bed of estate where the next royal birth would take place. My mother's bed! How dare Anne? How dare my father! From the looks of Anne, bloated and sallow, the birth was imminent.

"So," Anne said in a shrill voice, "Lady Mary has arrived."

I stood stock still. Lady Mary! Not "Princess Mary" or at the very least "madam," but a title that was no title at all, as though I were the daughter of the lowest, most impoverished baron instead of the daughter of the king of England.

Anne's onyx black eyes glittered in her pallid face. "Have you no manners?" she demanded. "Then we shall have to teach you some! Kneel!"

I hesitated. This was the first time Anne and I had come face-to-face, the first time Anne had spoken to me directly since the night of my now-abandoned betrothal to the French king. I had been only a child of nine then and had understood nothing.

Slowly I sank to my knees.

Anne glared at me. "I have only contempt for you, Mistress Mary. You and your wretched, scheming mother.

You are nothing but a bastard, you know—a mistake! The king's mistake. But now the king has corrected his error. His one true heir lies here, with me"—she stroked her huge belly—"and within a matter of days the future king of England will be brought forth. And you shall be his servant. I think that will be a good lesson for you, changing his napkins and cleaning up his messes. It will teach you your place in the world."

"And if it is a daughter, madam?" I asked. Immediately I regretted my boldness. I knew it was a mistake as soon as the words had left my mouth.

A silver goblet that had stood on a table at Anne's side flew past my head and clattered to the floor. Red wine splashed everywhere. I scarcely blinked.

"It is a son! It is a son!" Anne screeched.

Doomed Queen Anne

She risked *everything* to become queen

Though born without great beauty, wealth, or title, Anne Boleyn blossomed into a captivating woman. Without friends, and jealous of her sister's position in the English court, Anne used her wiles to win the heart of England's most powerful man: King Henry VIII. But she was not satisfied with only the king's heart. Anne was determined to replace Queen Catherine as his wife . . . and be crowned queen of England. So she promised Henry she'd do the one thing Catherine could not— bear him sons.

Anne persuaded Henry to defy his court, his religion, his family, and his subjects to crown her queen. But she didn't count on the one thing that would leave her completely and utterly alone: She could control Henry, but she could not control her fate.

Carolyn Meyer's third novel in the award-winning Young Royals series tells Anne's fascinating story in her own voice—from her life as an awkward young girl to the dramatic moments before her death.

Turn the page for a glimpse at the peril of Anne's bid for the throne. . . .

ONE MIDSUMMER EVENING as I supped in the maids' chambers, only half listening to their ceaseless chatter, a royal page appeared. The maids fell silent as the boy delivered to me a note. Written in French, it bade me come at once; it was signed *Henricus Rex*—Henry the King—and bore the king's seal.

He wanted me *now*. I had no opportunity to change my gown, arrange my hair, or do any of those things which a lady might wish to do in preparation for such an interview, no time to become unnerved by this new course I sensed my life was about to take.

I followed the young page, not to the king's privy chamber, as I had expected, but to an even more private chamber beyond it. King Henry sprawled at his ease behind an enormous table. It appeared that he had been playing draughts, for there was the black-and-red checkered board, but no sign of an opponent. The chamber was empty, save for the king and me.

I dropped to one knee, advanced, dropped a second and then a third time, reverencing the king as he required. "Your Majesty," I murmured, my eyes lowered modestly. This was the first time I had been alone with him. Slowly I raised my eyes and waited, my heart racing.

King Henry leaned toward me, his elbows on the table, his blue eyes lively, his smile winning. "Lady Anne." He breathed my name as though it were a sigh.

"Your Majesty," I said again, still kneeling. I allowed his gaze to wander over me from head to foot.

"You do please me greatly," said King Henry, and raised me up.

"It pleases me much to please you, your Majesty," I replied.

"Good," he said. "And would it please you just as much to be the king's mistress?" he asked, stroking his close-trimmed beard.

There was no mistaking his meaning, and I had long prepared myself for just such an invitation.

I also understood that, should I yield, I would immediately lose my advantage. I knew well what became of the king's former mistresses—my sister, for one; Bessie Blount, for another: When he tired of them, as he always did, they were discarded and then married off to a willing courtier. I was certain that many ladies had been approached in this manner by the king; I doubted that any had either the desire or the will to refuse what he asked of her. Who would have dared?

I did.

I dared because I wanted so much more from King Henry. I wanted the love of his heart and his soul, which I knew would be much harder to win. Once again I was a little girl on a storm-tossed ship, bound for an uncertain future—frightened, but also exhilarated.

Now I drew a careful breath and replied with feeling, "It flatters me to believe that Your Majesty thinks so highly of me. But surely Your Majesty understands that it is no small thing that he asks. My virtue and my honor are of the greatest value to me, and I cannot risk the loss of them."

My heart was hammering loudly as I made this bold claim of virtue and honor. I clasped my hands to still their shaking and waited for the king's response.

King Henry stared at me in amazement. "Are you *spurning* me, Lady Anne?"

I was trembling, but my voice remained strong. "Spurn the wishes of my king? Never! Surely, I could wish for no higher honor than the undeserved attentions of the handsomest and most godly man in all Christendom! But, I must weigh the cost to my reputation. I beg you, my lord, give me time to think on it."

"Then I bid you good night, madam!" said the king brusquely. "We shall talk another time."

"Nothing would please me more, Your Majesty," I murmured, and repeated the ritual, kneeling three times as I backed out of the king's chamber. As I ran through the several passageways on my way back to the maids' apartments, I could not help smiling to myself. The score: Lady Anne, one point; King Henry, naught.